Book Three of *A Lady Thea Mystery*.

First edition: July 2022.

ISBN: 978-1-7347202-9-7 (paperback)
ISBN: 978-1-7347202-8-0 (e-book)

Published 2022 by Celestial Pen Books.

ACKNOWLEDGMENTS

Thank you to:

My parents who support and believe in me.

Lynn Morrison, Audrey, and Jerri for all of your help and support.

Everyone who has been supportive of me.

And all that have followed Lady Thea's journey.

DISCLAIMER

This book mentions people and events from previous books.
For the best reading experience read:

An Invitation to Tea: A Historical Romance Novella
Book 1: Murder on the Flying Scotsman
Book 1.5: The Unread Letter
Book 2: The Corpse at Ravenholm Castle

———————

For a list of characters in this novel, please see Characters in the back of the book.

CHAPTER ONE

1910, LONDON

After being away for so long, Lady Theodora Prescott-Pryce was glad to be home. Prescott House was always going to be the place she was most happy to return to no matter how long she was away.

Thea closed her eyes and took a deep breath. It was strange to think that when she had left there, everything was so different. She felt different.

Barely two months ago, Thea had boarded the Flying Scotsman to visit her cousins at Ravenholm Castle in Scotland. She had been traveling with her maid, Molly Forbes, and wanted nothing more than to live her life in peace and quiet. She knew she would have to marry eventually, but she hoped to find a quiet marriage with a husband who would leave her be. She loved reading about adventures but never thought she would step into one.

On the train, she met Wilhelmina Livingston, who had been married to the awful older Livingston son, Ernest. Ernest killed a maid at Ravenholm Castle five years ago and possibly killed others, all in the name of a treasure that was found and sold centuries ago. Before Thea left Scotland, she heard that

Mr. Livingston had died of a heart attack in his prison cell. In a way, Thea was relieved that her friend wouldn't have to suffer the ordeal of her husband's trial.

She had also met someone on the train who claimed to be her half-brother. James Poyntz worked for his uncle's newspaper and had a relatively happy life, from what Thea had been able to gather with Detective Inspector Leslie Thayne's help. Thea had met the inspector on the train as well, and rather enjoyed his company. He had become a good friend, but she also blushed thinking about him and how he sometimes made her feel. Which was silly, since she had only known him for a short time.

James said he was the son of Thea's American mother and a retired English colonel turned novelist. From what Detective Thayne managed to uncover, her mother had given birth to James away from London before returning to marry Thea's father, the former Earl of Astermore.

Being home, she planned to confront her mother about this. She needed to know what the whole story was. James' guesses made for a pretty picture of a young couple in a forbidden romance.

But she also wasn't sure how much she could trust James. Her maid at Ravenholm, Bridget, had found photos of him abroad with a blackmail letter from Mr. Livingston about James being a spy. She needed to know what the true story was.

"Are you all right, my lady?" Bridget Semple asked. Bridget had agreed to be Thea's new maid, with everything that entailed, including coming to London.

"It's just strange being back."

Thea knew it hadn't been so long since she left, but it felt like a lifetime ago.

She climbed up the stairs. Mr. Morgan, the butler, opened the front door for her.

"My lady! Welcome home."

"Thank you." She smiled. "Is my mother home?"

"She's in the sitting room."

Thea inclined her head, but before she could take another step further into the house, the sound of tiny paws ran up, and she was greeted by the tiny feet of Artemis and Apollo, her mother's Blenheim Spaniels. Her kitten Mercury hissed jealously from her coat pocket as Thea knelt to rub the puppies' heads.

"They're nothing to worry about," she told the kitten, and she stroked his ears. She pulled him out of her coat pocket and handed him to one of the maids, Nellie, who was passing by. "Will you please feed him?"

"Yes, my lady. Oh, he's precious!" she cooed once the kitten curled into her arms. "What's his name, if you don't mind me asking?"

"Mercury."

"Oh, you must be quite fast for a name like that." She scratched behind his ears, and Mercury purred happily.

"Actually, he's a little thief, so don't let him around anything shiny."

Nellie laughed. "Of course, my lady. I'll take him downstairs to eat."

She nodded and watched as Nellie took him away.

Thea took a deep breath, steeling herself. She had learned a lot about her mother while she was away. Confronting her for the first time since felt nerve-wracking.

Her mother, the Dowager Countess Vivien Prescott-Pryce, sat on one of the low sofas near the window, reading an American newspaper that Thea believed her uncle had stock in. Dressed in a tea-gown, it was clear she wasn't expecting company.

A large fire roared in the fireplace, making the sitting room quite warm. Or perhaps Thea was just warm. She wanted to run back out and pretend nothing had changed.

No, she told herself and thought of James and of Colonel Bantry. The Colonel had pined for his lost love for decades, and James said he just wanted to know his family. If she had been in his shoes, she would want to know them also.

"Hello, Mother."

Her mother lowered the newspaper, face lighting up as she saw Thea.

"I didn't think you were coming home until Thursday."

"It is Thursday."

She wanted to shake her head. How had her mother managed to lie for so many years when she couldn't keep track of the days of the week?

She wanted to ask her about James, but another part of her didn't want to upset things before she had settled into the house again. She was ashamed to think that she listened to that part.

"How was your trip home?" Her mother asked. "Hopefully, no more murders."

"No more murders. No bodies at all." Thea took a seat opposite her mother. "It was nice."

"Good. Molly's settled in upstairs. I thought she might make use of the nursery when the baby arrives."

Thea nodded. It would be nice to still have her friend there. She hoped that Molly might get along with Bridget and that she wouldn't feel like Bridget had replaced her.

She had last seen Molly in Scotland when she traveled up there with Detective Constable Patrick Cooke. He had been undercover at the time, and his assignment had been to expose corruption in the Leeds Police department.

Molly's husband, Daniel Talbot, had been killed on the train to Scotland. His business partner's wife, Mildred, killed Daniel, and then her father, a police detective, had covered up the murder and framed Molly. Thea hadn't been able to return in time for their trial, so she hoped that Molly was doing all right.

"How has she been?"

Though they had written, Thea suspected that Molly censored her letters rather thoroughly to keep her from worrying. It would be just like her to do that.

"She's been a bit shaken up. Being a mother is daunting. Being a mother alone is far more so." Her mother took a breath. "She's been adapting the best that she can to what is normal now for her. I know she had an incident with her mother a few weeks ago, but she is spending time with her mother-in-law and father-in-law. She's gone to dinner at their home a few times."

Thea nodded. "I'm glad. She was so upset after what happened."

She nearly groaned as soon as the words were out of her mouth, and she buried her face in her hands. Of course Molly was upset. She stumbled across her husband's body with him brutally murdered. She was going to be alone to raise her and Daniel's child.

Well, not completely alone. She would have Thea, Thea's mother, Daniel's parents, and the servants in the house. Wilhelmina would love to act as a sort of aunt. From what Molly had written of Lionel Fletcher—her husband Daniel's former business partner—he seemed to have some level of interest in the child.

On the other hand, from what she had heard of Molly's parents, she wasn't sure they would be so supportive.

"You should go upstairs and freshen up."

That sounded like a good idea. She would love to get out of these clothes, having been in them for most of the day. It would be nice to change into something more comfortable.

"We aren't doing anything special for dinner," her mother said as she stood. "Just a night in."

Thea nodded.

"Is Molly home?"

Her mother glanced at the clock on the mantle, a clock that her great-grandfather had brought there. "Not yet. She's usually home in another hour or so."

That would give her plenty of time to rest up before she saw her again. With that thought in mind, Thea stood and excused herself before she walked out the door of the sitting room.

CHAPTER TWO

THEA BARELY WAS OUTSIDE OF THE SITTING ROOM WHEN Bridget stepped forward.

"Did you ask her, my lady?" Bridget asked, her thick Scottish accent so much more pronounced away from the others who also spoke in the heavy brogue.

"I was going to." Bridget shot her a disbelieving look. "It's not that easy to accuse your mother of lying to you."

Truthfully, she didn't want to deal with asking her mother such questions. There was far too much unhappiness to unearth, and she felt afraid to address it. She closed her eyes for a second and took a breath. Asking about James' parentage felt a little like she was intruding on something that wasn't any of her business. If her mother had wanted her and Cecil to know, surely she would have told them at any point. On the other hand, Thea desperately wanted to know. What would it have been like if he had been raised with them?

Cecil was always too quiet. Perhaps a brother would have brought him out of his shell. Leslie and his older brother Josiah seemed very close, and Thea always hoped that her brother might grow bolder with age. When Father died, Cecil was barely sixteen. As much as he was an adult, he was still a child when he became the Earl of Astermore, and it had to be hard for him. He wasn't his only peer with a title, but he was the only one in his circle of acquaintances that held the title in their own right and not just as a courtesy title.

Bridget glanced around and dropped her voice before she spoke again. "You don't have to accuse her of lying, my lady."

It felt like she was anyway.

"I don't know Mr. Poyntz well, but he seemed as if he was genuine in his revelation. Nothing I found in his room suggested otherwise."

That was another thing she didn't want to think about... the fact that Bridget had searched James' room while he stayed at Ravenholm Castle for the shooting party and found a black-mail letter containing a photograph of James abroad. And while that meant little by itself, the letter heavily suggested that he was a spy in His Majesty's Service.

"I'll talk to Mother later about it," Thea said as she ascended the stairs. "Right now, all I want to do is get changed for dinner."

Inside her room, Thea looked around. The light mint green walls reflected the already lit lamplight. The curtains were shut tight, despite being on the third floor. The room had always been something of a refuge for her where she could retreat from the rest of the world.

Her mother wasn't always so quiet. She talked often, and as much as Thea loved her mother, she sometimes found her exhausting. Where did she get the amount of energy that she had? Her mother was one of the few people she had met, along with her Aunt Diana, who seemed to actually like being around people. But where her Aunt Diana was a calm, stable presence like still water in a lake, her mother was much more like a river just before it tumbled over a waterfall.

A knock on the door came and Bridget rushed to answer it. Nellie held Mercury in her arms. The poor thing was half asleep and let out a rather loud meow of protest as Nellie transferred him to Thea's arms.

"He was such a sweetheart, my lady."

"Was he around Artemis or Apollo at all? I don't think he likes them much."

Which was a shame. She was rather hoping the three would get along if they were going to be living under the same roof. Mercury hadn't seemed to have any issue around the hunting dogs at Ravenholm, but perhaps that was just because he knew that he was still going to be the center of attention with them.

"He was, my lady. He was such a perfect angel to them after he warmed up to them."

She sincerely hoped he hadn't tried anything. Despite their names, Artemis and Apollo were rather gentle souls with easily hurt feelings. She had once told them "not now" when they wanted their bellies scratched, and they had whimpered and cried for the rest of the day until Thea had sat down on the floor and scratched their bellies to their hearts' content.

Thea pressed a kiss on the kitten's head, setting him in the little burrow she made for him on the bed. He purred contentedly and closed his eyes.

"Good night, you silly thing," she whispered. She knew he wouldn't be able to hold out for long against the puppies.

Thea turned back to Bridget.

"If it's an informal dinner, I don't really need to be dressed up," she said as she eyed the emerald gown her maid had selected. It was definitely far too fancy for just the three of them. If her grandmother had been there, that would have been another matter. But since she was not, Thea preferred to wear something simple. "The blue is plainer."

It also was not a gown she would be likely to wear out of the house or with company. It had been in her wardrobe for as long as she could remember. The pale blue made her skin washed out and her hair dark, so she tried not to wear it where anyone would see her.

She hated how it made her look if she was being honest. She wasn't entirely sure why she hadn't gotten rid of it or given it away yet. Still, maybe it could have something done to it. The dress itself was just a net overdress. If she had the pale blue underdress replaced with something else? Dark blue, maybe? She would have to ask Molly's opinion now that she was a fashion expert, especially since she had chosen such lovely gowns for Thea to wear at Ravenholm. Perhaps the dress could have some new life.

For now, it would do with its washed-out pale blue on blue. She looked at herself in the mirror, watching the way her face looked. Her cheeks had a rosiness to them that they hadn't in the past. Her face looked like it belonged to someone else, someone who had a love for life and all that it entailed. Her hair had lightened in the time she had been outside at Ravenholm without a hat, and it actually made her skin look less pale, which in turn made the dress actually look nice on. The net overdress actually seemed to have a glow against her skin.

A new underdress would definitely work well for that.

The gong wouldn't sound downstairs for dinner. Mr. Morgan only did that when guests were present. Instead, Thea decided that she should find out which room Molly was in. It would be nice to see her before dinner and catch up before they went down.

"Bridget, can you find out where Molly's room is?"

"Of course, my lady."

She nodded and took off. Thea sat down at her desk. Her

letters had been severely neglected in the time that she had been preparing to travel, but she hadn't planned on answering any of them before she returned to Prescott House.

———

THEA WALKED DOWN THE HALLWAY TO WHERE SHE BELIEVED Molly was staying. After the baby was born, her mother had written in one of her letters, the baby would live in the nursery upstairs. Molly planned to hire a proper nurse for her child and intended to still work at Fletcher's after the baby was born.

The idea seemed ridiculous at first. A mother working when she didn't have to? It wasn't like Molly was poor, and she certainly didn't need to work to keep a roof over her head. But from the few letters Molly had written, she was certain that it was for the distraction it provided for her.

She closed her eyes and took a deep breath before she raised her hand to knock. The door creaked open and it was clear to her now that it had never been closed in the first place. How silly she must have looked.

But then she saw the reason why it hadn't been closed. Inside, hovering near the vanity, Margaret Forbes Talbot stood as she pulled off her gloves.

"Molly!" Thea cried, moving into the room despite not being invited. Her former maid looked up and Thea reached out to grasp her hands. "How are you doing?"

"I'm well, my lady."

"Thea," she corrected gently.

Molly smiled. "Of course, Lady Thea." They sat down in the chairs, Molly at the vanity and Thea at the desk. "Did you have a nice trip?"

"It was good. A bit exciting."

"And the handsome inspector?"

"Nothing. We're just friends." Molly smirked. "Honestly, just friends."

Mercury wandered into the room. Molly stared at the kitten. Mercury blinked back before crying loudly. By now, Thea knew her cue to pick him up.

"My lady, you're holding a cat." She said that like Thea wasn't fully aware of that fact.

"His name is Mercury."

Molly blinked.

"I didn't think you liked cats."

Thea shook her head. "I've never really gotten to know one before. My grandmother's cat does not count."

Her grandmother's cat, Arnold, was a bit spoiled by her grandmother and so he hated everyone but her. He had bitten Thea once and her skin was still scarred.

"How have you been settling in?"

Molly nodded. "Everyone has been so kind."

"And the store?"

Something flashed across her face. It was gone as quick as it came, but Thea saw it.

"What's wrong with the store?"

Molly grimaced. "The board doesn't want me in charge since I'm a woman in a 'delicate condition'." She scoffed. "Lionel has backed my claim but I'm afraid they'll do whatever they have to to get me out."

"So, what can you do?" Thea asked her as she watched Molly fret over a pile of papers she had clearly taken from the office.

"I can find Daniel's notes on accounting. Someone funneling money out. The police thought it was Lionel, but I asked Detective Cooke. You might remember him from the train?" Thea nodded. "I asked him if he could look into Lionel's finances. There's nothing there, and Lionel says it wasn't him. Apparently, Daniel told him about... that I was..."

Her hand rested on her stomach, and Thea understood. "Lionel said he wanted to do better after that. He felt like he was letting Daniel down with the gambling."

"So he quit gambling?"

Molly nodded. "Any time he thinks he's going to gamble, he's been coming over here, and the Countess beats him at cards. Barely."

"Huh."

"She's very good." Molly smiled.

"So Lionel has no reason to have you out?"

Molly shook her head. "If Lionel gets rid of me from the store, Daniel's shares revert entirely to his parents. And, the way Victoria Talbot, Daniel's mother, invested, she owned shares as well. With Daniel's shares, his parents would own a majority of the store."

"So they have a motive to want you out."

Molly fixed her with a glare.

"What happened to the papers Daniel had given you? The ones you gave to Inspector Thayne? Surely there must be something in there."

Molly froze.

"I forgot about them." She waved a hand. "With all the stress, it wasn't a very high priority. I wonder if I can get them back."

"I don't see why not. They're your property. And now that the trial's over, what would they need them for?"

It had been in the newspapers about the trial. Detective Inspector Stanton and his daughter Mildred Stanton Fletcher, who was Lionel's wife, had been found guilty. There was so much evidence against them that she had no idea how they wouldn't be found guilty. Evidence and the fact that Mildred Fletcher had attempted to murder Thea in front of a train full of witnesses. Her father hadn't been able to cover that up.

"It didn't matter much anyway," Molly told her. "Daniel

had the accounting ledger in a code only he and the accountant, Mr. Bexley, could read."

Thea blinked.

"I found the ledgers and the code, but it still makes little sense. There's too many pages missing. Maybe the ones from the police will help it make sense." Molly sat down. "I'll contact Constable Cooke. Perhaps he can help."

"Do you want me to talk to Inspector Thayne about them? He was on that case as well."

Molly shook her head. "It's probably nothing that'll help much. I'm just hoping that maybe it'll help me with it somehow."

"What happened to the accountant? The one who wrote the code?"

"He died a few weeks ago. Right before Daniel, actually." Thea went to speak, but Molly shook her head again. "I already looked into it. He had been complaining for a while that his chest hurt before he died. He didn't live the best anyway. It really doesn't come as much of a surprise that he died."

Perhaps she had read too many books, but the fact that the accountant died right before Daniel still struck her as suspicious. Was that what triggered Daniel? The timing of it all was just too convenient.

Molly shook her head. "I don't want to think about it tonight. We can go to the store tomorrow. Lionel and I are starting to plan out the Christmas displays. It was Daniel's favorite time of the year, and we wanted to do something special to honor his memory."

"I can't wait to see it."

Molly beamed.

"And the new winter line is coming. I hope they'll have arrived by tomorrow."

That would be nice. She had been hoping to buy a new

pair of gloves. The lining in her favorite autumn pair was beginning to wear through. Bridget had already taken a look at them, but had determined that there wasn't much she could do to fix them properly. It would be nice to look around the counters there and find some things.

She would have Bridget come as well. While most lady's maids took their mistresses' cast-offs, Thea had always liked buying Molly a few nice dresses for when she dragged Molly to a show or to friends' weddings or out to nice restaurants. Bridget owned few clothes from what she had seen, and it would be nice to buy her some clothes as well.

Perhaps she just liked to see others dressed nicely. It was one of the things she was looking forward to before Charlie's presentation next year.

Although, she also had the vaguest of ideas that some of her excitement stemmed from knowing the owner of the store. It was never so exciting to go shopping before, even if she did like seeing others in pretty things.

"I'll let you get ready for dinner," Thea told Molly as she stood. Molly nodded.

"I'll see you downstairs, my lady."

CHAPTER THREE

THE NEXT MORNING, THEA, MOLLY, AND BRIDGET HEADED into Fletcher's. Ezra, the chauffeur who worked at Prescott House, drove them there. He eyed the building suspiciously and Thea knew that Molly must have told him stories about what was happening at Fletcher's.

"Would you like me to stay nearby, Lady Thea?"

She shook her head. "We can get a cab home when we're done."

He bowed his head. "Yes, my lady."

The doorman at the store opened the door for them and greeted Molly with a "Good morning, Mrs. Talbot." The lift operator, a young boy, did the same, as had everyone else they passed on the way to the lift. It was strange to Thea how everyone seemed to know Molly in such a short time.

"You're very popular here," Thea observed and watched as Molly's cheeks flushed.

"I've just talked to them."

"You care about the company."

She nodded and Thea understood. It wasn't just a job to her. If it was, she could have given it up and done anything.

She could have remarried, once her mourning period was up, to a man with a large fortune. She could have gone abroad. She didn't have to stay.

But the way she lit up around the people that she said hello to, how she knew each person's name, she thought that perhaps Molly had found someplace that made her happy.

"I'm glad that you have this," she told her. If it was helpful to her, it was a good thing.

She closed her eyes as the lift doors closed, and they began their ascent up to the office area.

"I just need to do a few things in the office, and then I can give you a tour of the store."

The lift came to a stop and Molly stepped out. As they walked to the office door, they passed a man who was looking down.

"Mr. Turner," Molly called, and Thea watched as the man startled. He turned around, his eyes wide. "I was wondering if you have those meeting minutes prepared yet?"

He blinked. "I—yes, ma'am. I can go get them now."

He brushed past them and past the lifts.

She stared after him. "That was rather odd."

"He's not usually so jumpy."

Thea found that hard to believe. The man had the kind of posture of someone who was used to not being noticed. He disappeared into a door down the hall.

Molly frowned, then turned around. "He is always rather odd towards me, though. He's always in the board meetings taking notes. They keep scheduling emergency meetings to discuss the most pointless of things. Lionel thinks they're trying to drive me crazy. That they want to see how long before I snap."

Thea felt her brow furrow as they came up to a door. Molly's office was a small bright room. Large windows covered two walls, the opposite of most rooms at the townhouse. The room faced the street, and the room was rather light.

Thea walked towards one of the seats in the front of the desk.

"Molly! You're in already? I thought I saw you come in, but it's rather early, and you should really get some rest—" The man stopped short as he saw her. "Hello. I'm sorry." He glanced at Molly. "Am I interrupting something?"

Molly shook her head. "No. We were just talking." She looked to Thea. "Lady Thea, this is Lionel Fletcher." He bowed his head. "Lionel, this is Lady Theodora."

"It's a pleasure to meet you. I've heard a lot about you." He nodded to the paper on Molly's desk with James' story about the train still there, despite it being old news now. "And read about your adventures."

She smiled. "It's nice to meet you as well."

"Have you had the grand tour around the store yet?"

Molly flushed. "I was going to, but well…" She gestured to the large pile of paper there and all the things that needed to be done.

"If you'd like, I could take Lady Theodora downstairs and show her around."

"That would be lovely." Thea smiled. "You can get off your feet and I can get to know Mr. Fletcher better."

"Lionel," he corrected her with a grin. "Please, I insist."

She nodded. "Please call me Thea."

She wasn't sure why she said that anymore. Hardly anyone actually called her just Thea. "It wasn't polite," her grandmother would say.

She didn't mind when they called her Lady Thea, though. It felt more fond and less formal than Lady Theodora. Lady Thea was someone not afraid of anything, who was comfortable with her own skin and with the world. She liked who she was better than the scared girl who sat in her room reading instead of living.

For so long, she felt out of place in society. She didn't have the confidence of her friends among the other debutants who made their debuts the same year she had, nor of her cousin Stella.

This was better. She was happier now, even with the unrest of the situation with her mother and James. She should talk to her about it, but the thought of bringing it up was also daunting. She didn't really want to start a fight between her mother and her.

"Penny for your thoughts?" Lionel asked as they stepped into the hall.

"It's just strange being home."

"You've had an eventful past few weeks, I've heard."

She nodded. "I'm hoping things will be… well, not normal, but definitely quieter now that I'm home. I'm glad to be back."

He nodded. "I imagine so."

The hallway had more people than Thea ever expected to see in the office area of a department store. She had never given much thought to the inner workings of it, but she supposed it would take a rather large army of people to run a business of that size. Lionel smiled and greeted the people as they passed, and Thea was quite impressed how personable he was. From everything with the case against his wife and the trial transcripts that Leslie had sent her, she thought that he would be different. Meeker, lacking in ambition and personality. Mrs. Stanton Fletcher made him sound like a bit of a doormat, getting stepped all over by his more confident and able partner.

"So why should Molly be resting?" Thea asked as they reached the elevator. She didn't dare ask when her former maid was in earshot. She might scold her about being nosey, the way she had last night.

He glanced around, as if he was afraid that someone might overhear, and leaned in closer. "Someone threatened her yesterday when she was leaving. Pushed her against the wall. She didn't catch their face, but they told her she needed to leave Fletcher's."

Thea stiffened. "Was she hurt?"

"Shaken, more than anything, I think."

They fell quiet as the lift doors opened, and they stepped inside. Someone wanted Molly gone from the store badly. Her presence made them nervous, but had this been going on the whole time she had been there, or was this the first incident? If it was, what had changed? Could Molly have inadvertently uncovered something that made her presence so terrifying to them?

"How bad is it? The business with the board." Thea asked when they were downstairs and away from the others. "Molly has a tendency to understate things."

"I've come to realize that." He let out a soft laugh. "All the years I knew Daniel, he always talked about his quiet, sweet wife. He forgot to mention that she's as stubborn as can be." He shook his head. "It wouldn't be so bad, but there are seven spots. I hold one, Molly holds one, and Daniel's parents hold one. The other four members invested heavily early on. Two of them are rather old-fashioned and stuck in their thinking. They believe that a woman, especially one in Molly's condition, should be at home and not 'meddling in men's affairs.'" He scoffed, shaking his head.

"You don't want her out?" she couldn't help but ask. She knew Molly had said he didn't last night, but that changed nothing.

"How could I run a company like this by myself? I'm not Daniel. He would have been fine running things by himself. Me? I'm a people person. I can talk to the press and the others and present at meetings, but at the end of the day, I'm not much of a numbers man. I'm not very good at keeping money straight."

"I heard." Thea gave a little laugh. "My mother sweeps you under the table regularly, is what I've been told."

Lionel laughed. "It's definitely not my strong suit. But Molly, she's good with all those details. I know we have an accounting department, but she's found all sorts of inconsistencies in the last reports that went out."

She closed her eyes and took a breath. It was too easy to see it. Molly, looking through the papers and finding something that didn't fit quite right. No wonder why she was so curious and interested to find Daniel's accounting notes. She needed them if she was going to figure this out.

Thea just hoped they could figure it out before Molly was threatened again. Or worse, hurt. Because Molly was too selfless. She wouldn't take the risk of injury seriously. Thea hoped that the baby would temper some of those instincts and help her start putting herself first more. When she heard about Molly's progress at the store, she thought that's what had happened. But it didn't seem that way.

"Daniel would crawl out of his grave and haunt me if I let anything happen to her," Lionel said. "So if there's anything I can do to help. I don't want to see her hurt."

Molly had been right when she said Lionel cared about her as a friend now. He didn't seem very interested in running the company alone, the antithesis to so many who scoffed at a lady in charge.

"Do you want to see some of the things Molly's ordered for the winter season?" he asked. Thea nodded. Bridget followed behind them.

The lights were off in the storeroom, and he frowned. "That's odd."

He reached for the switch and they blinked against the brightness. Bridget was the first to gasp.

"My lady—"

A body lay on the floor in the storeroom. A young man, well-dressed. He had been hit over the head, she could see it clearly from the way his skull was smashed in on one side, and blood clumped his hair, but what was rather odd to Thea was the lack of blood.

Moving closer, she recognized the man from earlier, Mr. Turner, who was supposed to be preparing the meeting minutes for Molly. What was he doing down here?

She reached out and placed her fingers on his neck. He was still warm, but she couldn't feel any sign of his heart beating nor see his chest rise or fall.

"I think he's dead."

Lionel's face lost color.

"We need to call the police," she told him.

He nodded, his body shaking.

They moved out of the room and Thea glanced around. "Where is a telephone?"

"Uh," Lionel looked down the hallway. "That way."

"Are you all right?" She winced as soon as she asked the question. "I mean, can you walk?"

He nodded. "I'm all right. It was just a shock. Who would do such a thing?"

"You'd be surprised."

THE DETECTIVE ASSIGNED TO THE CASE WAS ABOUT INSPECTOR Thayne's age, perhaps a bit older. He had serious eyes that Thea thought looked rather old on his face.

"I'm Inspector Thomas Haddington," he introduced himself as he came over to Lionel and Bridget and her.

"Lionel Fletcher. I'm one of the owners." The inspector nodded. "This is Lady Theodora and her maid, Bridget. I was giving them a look at next season's fashion line when we found… um, when we found…."

"The body?" the inspector asked, and Lionel nodded, face paling again. "Perhaps you ought to sit down."

"Yes, very good." He all but collapsed in one of the nearby chairs.

He glanced at Thea and Bridget. "Are you both all right?"

Bridget nodded. Thea did as well. Somehow, after the last few months, it felt rather oddly ordinary. It wasn't a pleasant feeling.

The inspector looked at her again, his brow furrowing. "Oh. You're that Lady Theodora."

She blinked. "I beg your pardon?"

"I work with Inspector Thayne." He smiled. "I hope I'm not overstepping when I say he talks about you."

Heat rose in her cheeks. "Oh."

Truthfully, she hadn't spoken to Inspector Thayne since he left Ravenholm. They wrote letters, but it wasn't the same. He was working, though, and Thea knew how busy he had to be. She missed him and hoped that they could meet up soon.

"Nothing bad," he said in a rush as he realized how the words had to sound. "He seems very fond of you. Called you a lady detective. I'm not quite sure what that means. I've never met one of those before."

Thea thought about smiling, but it felt inappropriate considering what was happening.

"It's nice to make your acquaintance. I only wish the circumstances were better."

He nodded.

"Do you feel all right? We can postpone the interview…." He trailed off.

Thea watched Lionel. He seemed rather uncomfortable with the whole thing, and Thea couldn't blame him.

"That might be best," she said softly, glancing back to Inspector Haddington.

She looked over to him again and saw Lionel sway.

The inspector nodded. "I'll come by tomorrow, if that's all right?"

Lionel nodded. "Yes. Yes, tomorrow should be fine."

He walked away, and Thea turned back to Lionel. "Perhaps you ought to go home?"

Lionel shook his head. "I'll be all right. Just need some fresh air." He closed his eyes. "We should all get some fresh air."

Thea glanced back towards Bridget. "Actually, I think I'll speak with Molly and come back tomorrow."

Despite having seen bodies before, for some reason, seeing Lionel's reaction made it feel different.

———

THE HOUSE WAS QUIET WHEN SHE AND BRIDGET RETURNED home, and she vaguely remembered hearing her mother say she would be out this afternoon. It was just as well, Thea thought. She would like some quiet, some peace after the day she had had. For some reason, today, the sight of Lionel's discomfort struck her worse than the other times she had stumbled across a murder. Perhaps it was seeing someone else's reaction? With Daniel's murder, she hadn't truly understood what she had been seeing. With Kate's murder, she had been dead for so long that it hadn't felt real to her. She had been dead for so long that the body had been near unrecognizable.

"I'm going to rest," she told Bridget.

"Would you like help undressing, my lady?"

Thea nodded.

Upstairs, Bridget helped her peel off her skirt and shirt. She unlaced layers and hung them neatly. She pulled on a tea gown and waited for Bridget to shut the door behind her before Thea sat down at her desk and pulled out her journal.

She wasn't thrilled with finding another body. The last one she found led her to getting shot at a number of times. The one before that had her dangling from a train and held at knifepoint. Perhaps it was just the vulnerability of having trusted James, only to discover what she knew about him was a lie.

She flipped back to the first page in the journal where she had written about Daniel's case and pulled out a blank piece of paper. In her best handwriting, she began writing, though she had no real clue where she was going with it.

Still, it felt good to get it all out.

The words felt like they flowed, though. Her pen sailed across the paper, onto the next before a whole stack was filled. A knock at the door and Bridget's voice were the only thing that made her realize it was time to get dressed for dinner.

CHAPTER FOUR

MOLLY LOOKED TIRED WHEN SHE CAME OUT OF HER ROOM FOR dinner. From the dark smudges under her eyes, she seemed to have aged.

"I heard about what happened today," Molly said as they walked down the stairs into the dining room. "Inspector Haddington said he'll come by tomorrow to talk to Lionel."

Thea nodded. "I can be there."

Molly smiled at her, her hands clasped in front of her. "Thank you."

"I didn't even know him. I don't know why it's bothering me so much."

Molly reached out and squeezed her hand. "It just means you're human, my lady."

———

"PHONE CALL FOR YOU, MY LADY," MR. MORGAN SAID AS THEY left the dining room. "He said his name is Inspector Thayne."

A smile spread across her face as she walked into the hallway and picked up the phone. "Hello?"

"Thea?" Leslie's voice crackled through the other end.

"It's good to hear from you."

"Are you all right? I heard there was a murder at Fletcher's today and that you were there."

Thea nodded, even though she knew he couldn't see her. "I'm all right."

"What happened?"

"Lionel, er, Mr. Fletcher, was giving me a tour of the store. We went down to see the storeroom and found the body."

He paused on the other end. "So there wasn't anyone else?"

She shook her head. "Not that I saw."

Leslie let out a deep sigh. "Good. I don't want you to go poking around again, especially not by yourself." She could almost picture him staring at her, giving her that intense look. "I don't want you getting into any danger."

"I'll be careful."

He started to argue but must have realized that was as good as he would get her to promise. "Will you be going back to the store then?"

She nodded. "Tomorrow. I never got to finish my tour, and Molly plans to continue showing me around."

"I'll try to stop by then."

She couldn't help the way her face warmed. It wouldn't do to say how eager she was to see him again.

He was quiet for a long moment. "I look forward to seeing you."

"I do too. Goodbye."

She hung up the phone in a rush, dropping her head against the wall. She sounded so stupid. Perhaps it was the fact that she never spoke to people, specifically to any men she had any interest in. Her only consolation was that he had seemed just as awkward as her.

Molly stood in the doorway with a smirk. "Inspector Thayne?"

Thea glared, her eyes narrowing. "He wanted to see if we were all right after the murder."

Her expression darkened briefly at the mention of the murder. "That was very kind of him." Molly's hands clenched by her side. "If you'll excuse me, I'm quite tired."

"Of course. Good night. Sleep well."

Molly moved toward the stairs and Thea hoped she hadn't misstepped. There wasn't much that could be done though if she had. The day had been long and stressful and Thea couldn't wait for it to be over.

THE NEXT MORNING FOUND THEA AT FLETCHER'S AGAIN. Lionel was noticeably absent, though a note at the secretary's desk explained that he had taken the morning off.

Molly left earlier than Thea and had been at the store for several hours when Thea and Bridget arrived there. She said she wanted to be at the store early to deal with the aftermath of the day before. Thea couldn't help but worry about her, at least a little.

"I won't be able to show you around until the afternoon," Molly told Thea. "I had Miss Cooper call, but Mr. Morgan said you had already left the house."

"That's all right. We can find something to amuse ourselves."

The main showroom was quite grand. Counters with crystal displays, gloves and hats, and perfumes lined the floor. Salesgirls in black dresses manned the counters with the ladies' accessories and men at the men's counters.

Thea wandered the floor with Bridget a step behind her.

"Can I help you find something, my lady?" a salesgirl asked.

"A new hat, perhaps." She glanced back at Bridget. "What do you think?"

"A new hat would be very nice, my lady."

"And one for you as well. I insist," she added as Bridget began to argue.

"Thank you, my lady."

Thea saw the salesgirl make a face for the briefest of seconds, but it had been replaced by a pleasant smile by the time she turned back around. "Of course. Right this way, my lady."

She knew the girl didn't truly want to serve Bridget. Despite department stores catering to all classes, it wasn't the first time someone had been annoyed to serve both Thea and her maid at the same time. They only watched her reactions, never her maid's. Her likes, her dislikes. It made her feel uncomfortable sometimes.

She liked to be able to browse the counters without people asking her to make decisions quickly. Still, she followed the girl to the ladies' department and waited as the black-clad salesgirls swarmed around her with choices of bright, colorful hats. She was guided to sit as they brought over a variety of styles that were decisively not for her.

She liked one of the hats with many feathers. It was strange and unique and very tall and completely frivolous. She would probably never wear it out of the house but Mercury would probably love playing with the feathers.

"Perhaps the black with the bow, my lady," Bridget pointed. Despite having only been her maid for a short time, Bridget already seemed to know her preferences. In the mirror, one of the salesgirls pulled a face, quick enough that Thea might have never noticed if she hadn't been looking.

One of the girls brought over a black velvet hat. It had a

large dotted bow but was otherwise quite plain, but was a very attractive hat. Thea smiled and nodded her permission and the girl stepped forward and set it delicately on her head. She had a fondness for black outside of a mourning color. It added a layer of mystery to her, shrouding her in shadows and framing her face nicely.

"It's a lovely hat, my lady."

Thea nodded and the girl took it to the counter to add to her account. Long before she knew that Molly's husband owned Fletcher's, Thea had opened an account at the store where she had bought so many accessories. Her clothes had usually been custom-made, especially her evening wear, though if there were more gowns like what Molly had sent to Scotland, she could easily see herself buying more clothing from Fletcher's. Not every occasion required a dress custom made, and it would be good for Molly's business for people to be seen in her clothes.

The salesgirl who had brought over the velvet hat was helping Bridget pick out one as well. Nothing too showy, though, from what she saw her maid admiring.

AFTER BROWSING THE STORE, THEA WANTED TO TAKE ANOTHER look at the storeroom and she doubted that Molly would be amenable to that. The storeroom was below the actual store, but it didn't take much effort to find how to get down there without anyone noticing.

She wore her plainest suit that day, a navy blue wool one, that allowed her to blend into the background quite nicely. She didn't think anyone would stop them, especially not if they looked like they belonged there.

Leslie was right. Rushing in would get her nowhere. She shouldn't put herself in too much danger. She shouldn't keep doing that, repeating the same habit that both James and Leslie had warned her about.

She looked up at the door. Surely it wouldn't hurt to just take a look, though. No one was there.

She glanced back at Bridget, who seemed to be thinking the same thing.

"My lady, are you sure this is a good idea?"

She let out a breath.

"It's not the worst idea?" she offered. Bridget stared at her as if she was unsure that Thea hadn't lost her mind. The way Thea figured it, though, was that whoever killed the man wasn't likely to stay around.

Besides, she wasn't alone.

"I just would like to take a look around."

Bridget bit her lip but moved forward to unlock the door.

The first thing she noticed was the complete lack of blood. She noticed it yesterday, but it was still surprising. Kate had been murdered five years ago, so it had made sense to her at the time. But when Daniel had been murdered in her compartment, there had been enough blood to track it into the corridor. Here though, there was barely a spot on the ground, which was weird considering the way she found him.

It would have been hard to move someone of his size unnoticed, wouldn't it?

"Meow!"

Thea jumped as a cat brushed up against her leg. It had brown, black, and orange patches across his back and Thea knelt to run a hand across his head. "Where did you come from?"

He preened under her touch and meowed loudly again before he took off, running towards a door that was barely cracked open. Thea stood and looked at Bridget.

"Should we follow him, my lady?"

Thea nodded.

The room the cat ran into opened into another large storeroom. Thea glanced around hoping for some clue where to go next, when the cat meowed loudly again from the other side of the room, as if he was waiting for them to follow.

"There."

They walked quickly towards the cat, who sat there delicately licking his paw and looking like he hadn't a care in the world.

Thea deflated a little. She was so sure that following the cat would have led them somewhere. To something. She shouldn't even be trying to investigate anyway. She promised Leslie she would be careful and running around a storeroom where someone had been killed yesterday was hardly careful.

She knelt back down, offering her hand out to the cat. He butted his face against it and she moved slowly to scratch his ears.

"Where did you come from anyway?" she asked him in a soft voice. The cat meowed again, but she didn't really expect an answer. He must have gotten in somehow but she doubted anyone knew how.

Thea sighed and stood up. If only he could talk... She imagined he had to have seen all sorts of things. Perhaps he even saw who killed Mr. Turner or knew why they brought him into the storeroom.

As she straightened, she spotted a door she hadn't seen before. Hidden behind boxes and crates, it was really no wonder. Perhaps the cat did bring a bit of luck after all.

"Bridget!" she called back to her maid, "I've found something."

She pulled at the crates with all her strength. Bridget moved quickly to help her.

"Are you sure this is a good idea, my lady?"

"No." She let out a breath and yanked harder. The crates

slid and Thea let go. The door was locked, though that was hardly surprising. "Can you open this?"

Bridget nodded and Thea stepped aside to let her in. Inside the room, there was a lot of blood. Whatever she had been expecting to find, it hadn't been that.

She glanced around quickly, mindful to stay outside of the room. A metal pipe, crusted in blood, lay discarded on the floor.

"I think we found where he was killed."

She turned to look at Bridget, who stood rather pale.

"Do you think you can lock it again? Inspector Haddington should be here soon and he should see this."

CHAPTER FIVE

Inspector Haddington met her and Bridget in one of the empty offices upstairs after he spoke with Lionel.

"Did you know Mr. Turner?"

Thea shook her head. "I met him for a brief moment yesterday." She closed her eyes, thinking back. "Molly–Mrs. Talbot said he was unusually jumpy."

Now, she couldn't help but wonder if he had somehow known he was going down to his death.

"I know I shouldn't have been, but Bridget and I found something related to the case," she told him and watched as the man stared at her from across the table. She leaned forward. "We found where I believe Mr. Turner may have been killed."

His eyes widened slightly. "Inspector Thayne had mentioned your tendency to find things."

That was putting it quite kindly. Since Inspector Thayne had known her, she had found trouble in most cases. She didn't want to, but it seemed to find her anyway.

"Will you show me where?"

Thea nodded. "Of course."

They made their way downstairs, ignoring the curious looks that followed them as they went. Thea took a breath and kept her eyes forward as they stepped into the elevator. She heard the inspector tell the boy operating the lift to take them downstairs. Bridget shuffled in beside her and kept close.

"So tell me, how exactly did you come across the room?" the inspector asked, sparing a glance at the elevator boy who kept his eyes on the door.

"It sounds silly, but there was a cat." The inspector blinked. "He led me through to another room and I happened to spot the door. Bridget picked the lock to the room. We only found it by chance. Someone had moved some crates in front of the door."

They had moved the crates back before they left. She hoped that it would hide the door and not let the killer know that the room had been found, if they still happened to be there.

The elevator reached the correct floor and the boy pulled the door open for them. The inspector held out his hand, motioning for Thea to go first. She stepped out into the hall. Bridget followed her and the inspector after them. They reached the door of the storeroom and Thea led the way to the other room where they had found the blood.

"It's behind there," she told the inspector, motioning to the wall of crates.

He pulled at the crates and Bridget stepped up to help Inspector Haddington move them. With the door open, she heard him inhale sharply from where she stood.

"I do believe you may be right, my lady. I believe this was where he was killed."

Thea let out a breath.

For the briefest of seconds, when she turned, she thought she saw Mr. Turner's face in the glass of the storeroom window. His eyes were wide, and his face was smudged with dirt that didn't match his otherwise pristine suit.

Thea blinked, but he disappeared. It didn't make any sense, though. She didn't believe in ghosts so there had to be a rational explanation.

"My lady, are you all right?" Bridget asked. She stared at her face. "You're very pale."

"I thought I saw… but that's silly."

It didn't make any sense. Ghosts weren't real. When she thought a ghost was haunting Ravenholm by stealing her things, it turned out to be Mercury. So there had to be some way to make sense of this as well.

But men didn't wear dead men's faces.

"My lady?" the inspector asked gently as he stepped towards her.

"He—it was outside. I'm not even sure what I saw. Perhaps my mind playing tricks on me."

Bridget stared concerned at her, "It's quite late in the day. Perhaps you're hungry, my lady?"

Thea nodded. "Yes…" She took a breath. "Yes, I suppose you're right."

"I didn't mean to take up so much of your time, my lady." He bowed his head. "I'll let you be going now."

Bridget waited until they made it back into the store before she spoke again.

"If you don't mind me asking, my lady, what did you see that spooked you so?"

"I thought I saw Mr. Turner."

"Mr. Turner? The dead man?" Bridget stared at her in horror. "You don't think Fletcher's is haunted, do you?"

"No!" She ducked her head as people glanced in their direction. "No," she repeated in a quieter tone. "I do not think that Fletcher's is haunted. I think there has to be a reason for this. Perhaps someone who just looked like him. I didn't get the best look at the man, after all."

Bridget opened her mouth to speak, but no words came out.

"I shouldn't have said anything. It's completely ridiculous."

She could barely keep her voice from trailing off as she saw the man cross the store floor and move towards the stairs with a surprising amount of speed for a dead man.

Instead, she forced a smile on her face. The very thought of a ghost would spook Bridget for good. "I'm sure it's nothing." Bridget seemed skeptical but didn't argue. Still, Thea felt the need to add, "Just my mind playing tricks on me."

CHAPTER SIX

"THEA!" JAMES CRIED WHEN HE SAW HER IN THE CAFE WHERE Bridget had left her. It was Bridget's first time really getting to look around a department store and Thea noticed her eying more than one of the displays. She finally had to tell her to go look. She supposed it probably wasn't easy to shop for yourself with your employer standing over your shoulder.

Thea smiled at James. The last time she saw him was in Ettrick Bay, when he had gotten her and Wilhelmina and Thea's cousin Charlotte front row spots to watch Mr. Baird's plane go up. The flight had been short, but Thea could see why Charlie wanted to see it so badly, even though she had never understood her cousin's obsession with flying machines. She supposed it was like her cousin Stella's interest in cars.

James stopped in front of her table. "I didn't expect to see you here today."

She smiled and motioned to the empty seat that Molly had abandoned. James pulled out the chair and sat down, helping himself to the sandwiches and tea.

"Have you been keeping out of trouble?"

"Of course."

His eyebrows raised into his forehead and he paused his actions. "Now, why do I completely not believe that?"

"I don't go looking for trouble. Trouble finds me, usually."

James chuckled. "I definitely don't believe that. Who was out exploring abandoned towers alone?"

The tower ruins he was talking about were the faux ruins that were built centuries ago by one of the former Earls of Ravenholm to hide their jewels. On the outside, the tower served no purpose. However, on the inside, it had a hidden compartment that had been used to store some of the family's fortunes, and later, by Mr. Livingston to hide a body. The jewels Mr. Livingston had been looking for had long been sold to help keep the Ravenholm fortune going. "It wasn't abandoned. It was a folly."

"The only folly was you exploring it unsupervised," he said with no real heat. "The minute you're alone, you find bodies and murderers and nearly get killed. It's not a very good way to live long."

She closed her eyes. "I know."

It wasn't like she had a death wish or was an adventure seeker. But she hadn't been lying when she said that trouble just sort of kept finding her.

"So, what brings you to Fletcher's?"

"I'm writing a fluff piece." He rolled his eyes. "My uncle thinks I'm getting into too much trouble. That I'm supposed to just report things and not get involved in the story." He shook his head. "As if I could standby and watch anything like that happen."

"You didn't have to, though. Inspector Thayne was there too. He could have handled it."

James shrugged as he took a sip of tea. "Just the right place at the right time, I guess."

He didn't sound convinced by his own words. She could

hardly blame him. He wasn't just in the right place at the right time by chance. He made sure to put himself there.

She couldn't help but remember the photographs of him. Were those just coincidences too? Just the right place at the right time? Or was there something more sinister there too?

She didn't want it to be anything more sinister.

Though she hadn't known him long, she had grown to care for him deeply.

Growing up, Thea had always hoped for someone to play with. Cecil was a serious child, always very deep in his own head or reading. Going to Scotland to visit Charlie and Anthony was a refuge from the mundane. Cecil used to stay in the library for most of those trips, never wanting to venture beyond the house into the sunlight.

Father used to encourage them to get fresh air, so she used to go outside and daydream about what it would be like to have another sibling.

At school, she had been encouraged to be a proper lady and she had worn that facade like an ill-fitted coat. While she wanted to be proper, she found it had become stifling to give up her freedom. And all the while, she always thought that it would have been so much easier if she had been born as a son instead of a daughter.

From hearing James speak, that was clearly not the case. He was just as restricted as her, only his restrictions looked different than others. On top of that, she had been graced with an open-minded and rebellious American mother, who had encouraged Thea to do what she would like, within reason. When Thea inherited her aunt's fortune, it gave her a considerable amount of freedom that others, including her brothers, didn't have.

"Are you in London for long?"

James nodded. "For the winter, at least. My aunt and uncle don't like traveling once the snow starts."

"That's understandable."

"And you? Will you be in London long?"

She took a sip of tea to clear her throat. "We close Prescott House in November. Mother likes to spend Christmastime at Astermore."

"That's in Yorkshire, isn't it?"

She nodded.

"I'm sure you'd be welcomed to join us there, if you'd like."

She watched him swallow hard, his eyes almost glassy for a moment. He blinked and looked away for a second. When he spoke again, his voice was heavy and full of something she couldn't easily name. "Thank you. But I'm not sure that would be a very good idea."

"Why not?"

"I… Thea, I adore you, and I care deeply about our friendship."

"But…?"

"But I don't know if it's such a good idea for me to insert myself into the rest of your family's lives."

"They're your family too, though."

He shook his head, something sad in his eyes that didn't make it to the rest of his face. "They're not. I don't know them."

Her throat felt a bit tight. It sounded like an excuse more than anything. She could hear what he refused to say. He was afraid. And while she wasn't sure if she could trust him fully, not after the letter that Bridget had found hidden in his room at Ravenholm that accused him of being a spy, he had also saved her life and had shown that he did care about her. And despite her better judgment, she did want him to be part of her family's lives. She wanted him to spend Christmas with them at Astermore and meet his niece and Cecil and Ilene, and their mother.

But she could understand being afraid of not belonging. It

was part of why she had tried to keep to herself, for the most part.

She reached across the table and took his hand, squeezing it. "I won't push the issue." At his disbelieving look, she amended, "for now."

He nodded, a smile starting to come to his lips. "Yes, that sounds more like you."

Thea laughed. She would let the issue rest for now, but not forever. She wanted to talk to her mother about it first before she broached the subject with James again.

After tea, Thea returned to Molly's office. While Molly had work to do, her former maid was more than happy to let Thea read, while Bridget took their purchases back to Prescott House with Ezra. It was a surprise to see Detective Constable Patrick Cooke again. What was more surprising was that he approached Molly in her office with little thought, as if he had done it a million times.

"I heard what happened. I hope you don't mind that I stopped by."

Molly shook her head. "Not at all. Thank you for coming."

Thea watched as Molly glanced down at the desk, shuffling papers with the same nervous tick that she used to clean Thea's room when she was hiding something.

"Are you... I also heard you were attacked the other night."

Molly shook her head again. "It was nothing."

Constable Cooke clenched his hands, tightening and then loosening his fingers. He caught sight of Thea from where she had stood in the corner.

"Lady Theodora," he greeted. "I didn't realize you were here. What a pleasant surprise."

Thea smiled. "It's nice to see you again, Constable. Hopefully, in the future it's under better circumstances."

"Agreed."

He turned his eyes to Molly again. "Are you sure you're all right? I can ask for a constable to be posted here."

Molly smiled. "I'm grateful for your concern, but it was really nothing."

"There was a dead body downstairs that says otherwise."

Thea watched as Molly went stiff. Her shoulders tensed and her head jerked up.

"Did you know him well?"

Molly took a deep breath, closed her eyes, then shook her head. "I've seen him at board meetings. He worked for Mr. Hervey, who has been rather insistent on my immediate retirement."

"Retirement?" Thea asked. That didn't sound like the dismissal that she knew some of the others were asking for.

"He wanted me to keep my shares but not have any voting rights, and to step back completely. I would have no control over the company." In a soft voice, she added, "Daniel's company."

Constable Cooke's brow furrowed. "I thought your husband and Mr. Fletcher were business partners?"

Molly scoffed. "Lionel cares very little for the business side. He's good enough at it, but after everything that happened, he doesn't trust himself with it."

"And you don't either."

Molly shook her head again. "I trust him. But there's very little difference between Lionel and people who drink a little too much or use morphine or do other things that they know are bad for them, but can't help themselves."

His brow furrowed. "You're saying he's an addict?"

"It's how Lionel described himself. Daniel noticed, when he

was alive… sometimes Lionel would act off. He would lie about what he was doing. He would ask Daniel for money out of the blue. He always asked, never stole it from him. But Lionel's father did the same, from what I've been able to piece together. He lost their house playing cards, and Lionel's mother took Lionel and his brother to live with her sister and her family when they were younger. That's how he met Daniel. His aunt paid for him to attend the same school as Daniel. She said that there was something wrong with his father and a good education was the only way to solve it." Molly closed her eyes. "His aunt is good friends with my parents. They share similar viewpoints of the world."

Constable Cooke nodded in understanding and Thea wondered if the constable had ever met Molly's family. Everything Thea had heard about them left her with a sour taste in her mouth. From Molly's letters while she was in Scotland, they sounded entirely unpleasant, and she was very glad that they were low enough in society that she had never met them before.

He bowed his head. "My apologies for barging in, my lady."

"Not at all." She smiled at him and stood as she saw Bridget standing in the doorway. "I was going to head home." She looked at Molly. "I'll see you for dinner. It was nice to see you again, constable."

DESPITE WHAT SHE TOLD JAMES, THEA HAD NO DESIRE TO WAIT before confronting her mother about James. The longer she put it off, the less likely she was to do it and the more likely she was to lose her nerve completely. It felt too strange to ask, but she needed to know. She needed the confirmation. She needed something.

She found her mother in the drawing-room, standing by the window as she read a letter.

"Cecil wrote," her mother said as Thea entered the room. "Ilene is pregnant again. They're hopeful it'll be a boy this time."

Thea sat down on the sofa, her head feeling a bit light.

"That's lovely. I'm very happy for them." She found she almost meant the words when she spoke them. It wasn't exactly a secret that she and her sister-in-law had a tumultuous relationship at the best of times. If only Ilene could have married someone else, perhaps they could have remained friends. It felt childish to even think it, but she hadn't been the one to push so far away. She missed Ilene and she loved her niece dearly, but when Zoe was born, she felt at family events as if she was the spinster aunt who needed others' charity to survive.

Her mother sighed, moving to sit across from her. "Oh, my darling, I wish you would find someone. I do wish to see you happy and settled."

Thea bit her tongue. It wasn't the first time marriage had been brought up, but usually it only happened around the Season or when her mother got it in her head that Thea was going to wind up all alone. It was rare and she shouldn't be so hurt to hear it, but it stung to hear that she had disappointed her mother.

"I am happy." It wasn't a lie. She liked her life as it was now. "And I met someone I'd like to ask you about."

"Oh?"

"Not like that." She glanced down, looking at her hands as she played with the edge of her dress. "His name is James Poyntz."

The words fell out of her mouth without permission and the effect was instantaneous. Her mother froze, going stiff as a statue. Slowly, she turned to face Thea.

"What did you say?"

Thea licked her lips. "James Poyntz."

"How do you know that name?"

"I met him on the train and then he came to Ravenholm with his aunt and uncle. He claimed he was my brother." Her mother stayed silent and it spoke louder than anything she could have said. But Thea still wanted to hear her say it. "Is James Poyntz my brother?"

"Why did he approach you?"

"He said he wanted to see if I was happy. He wanted to know me." She watched as her mother sat down on one of the sofas. Her shoulders had never looked so heavy. "He said Father approached him years ago." Thea sat down beside her mother. "He said that Father said that he would have raised him as his own if he had known about him."

Her mother slumped. Her shoulders fell and she let out a shaky breath. "I loved him. I tried not to get too attached knowing that I'd have to give him up. But when I held him in my arms, I loved him."

How hard must that have been for her.

"He would like to meet you." Her mother took a deep breath. "Would you want to meet him?"

Her mother shook her head. "I don't know. Perhaps."

"Why did you never tell Cecil or me about James?" She reached up, running her fingers through the pieces of hair that had fallen loose.

"There never seemed to be a good time."

"But—"

"My parents were… traditional, to say the least. They wanted my sister and me to marry wealthy, titled husbands. My father had built an empire, one that would go to my brother, Harold."

Thea nodded. She had vague memories of her uncle Harold, most of them being from her cousin Stella's wedding to the Earl of Wraughtley a couple of years ago. He was a stern man and she could certainly understand how her mother's father could be as well.

"I tried to be a good daughter. I came to London with my mother. I was prepared to marry someone I had never met or barely knew. And then I met Stephen." Her mother let out a sigh. "He had a way of seeing the world that was truly beautiful. The way only an artist could, only he painted with his words."

She shook her head, as if to clear it, but Thea knew exactly what she meant. She loved Colonel Bantry's writing. It portrayed the beauty in the world and she adored the escape from reality it provided.

Her mother sighed and continued. "We were young and in love. I met your father and he was just… he wasn't Stephen. At that point, I couldn't have seen myself with anyone else. But your father had a title which made my mother happy, and on paper the Prescott-Pryces were well off, which made my father happy. When they decided I would marry him, I was already with child." Her hand dropped to her stomach, eyes far off. "Matthew was so understanding about all of it. It hurt my heart how much he was willing to accept everything. He told me he would claim the child was his, but I couldn't do that to him, especially not if it had been a son. It would have cheated any of his sons of what was theirs. So I asked him for time. And I gave James away." She closed her eyes. "I didn't name him. I didn't even know what his name was until Matthew approached me with it all those years ago. I think he knew that I would never look for him, that I couldn't ask to be part of the life of a child I had abandoned."

Thea never questioned if her mother loved her father. She always knew her parents loved each other. It was evident in everything. But she also didn't think her father would be happy watching her mother punish herself for something that happened so long ago. He had clearly wanted James to be part of their family. So it would only be right to respect her father's wishes and include him.

Her mother would never take the first step. Thea was positive that approaching her had been all the more risk James was willing to take in this instance. He would rather risk life and limb to protect her, but for something he so clearly wanted, to know his family, terrified him.

"Would you be opposed to me inviting him for dinner? Not tonight," she added quickly as her mother began to protest. "In the future sometime. I'd let Mrs. Green know beforehand, of course."

Her mother nodded, though her eyes conveyed her uncertainty. "I supposed that would be all right."

CHAPTER SEVEN

THE NEXT DAY, THEA DECIDED SHE WOULD GO BACK TO THE store. It was one of the few places she could go without drawing too much attention to herself as a young, unmarried woman. Her reputation would pay if she went traipsing around all of London without a chaperone, but she refused to get her mother involved in a murder. She wasn't in the country or with a police officer that she could easily claim had told her she had to come with him.

Wandering around the store's main floor, it was something of a surprise to see Leslie Thayne again.

"Thea," Leslie smiled. "It's good to see you again."

She smiled. "You too. You look well."

"So do you."

She wasn't sure why it felt so awkward to see him in person again. Perhaps because one of the last times she saw him, she had been eavesdropping on his conversation with Inspector Anderson when he had been at Ravenholm Castle. They were discussing James' probable guilt at the time, at least, that's what Thea had thought. Still, she felt guilty for spying on him.

Mostly, she felt embarrassed about almost kissing him when

they were alone in the library. Should she have kissed him? Stella would have, but Stella was a different type of person than she was. Her American cousin was bold in ways she had never been. Defiant.

She wished she could be braver too.

"I've enjoyed getting your letters," she told him.

They were the highlight of her day when the mail arrived and a letter from Leslie was in it.

"So did you come here because of the murder?"

He shook his head. "I'm not on this investigation. Besides, it's in good hands with Inspector Haddington." His eyes trailed over her face, as if he was looking for something. "I wanted to see if you and Mrs. Talbot were all right. I heard she was assaulted the other day as well."

Thea nodded. "Lionel—Mr. Fletcher, that is—said she didn't want to call the police. It would make her look weak."

Leslie frowned. "Because she's a woman?"

"There's been some issues with the board of directors. They're reluctant to accept Molly. Between her age and her being a widow who is about to be a mother, they're afraid."

"Enough to attack her, do you think?"

She shook her head, glancing around to check for eavesdroppers before she spoke. "I have no idea. I haven't met any of them. Although Daniel's parents hold one seat, as I understand it. Lionel holds another."

"I don't want to step on any toes with the investigation, but I'll definitely keep an ear out. But Inspector Haddington is an excellent detective. I learned a lot from him."

"You respect him."

Leslie nodded. "I do." He smiled at her. "Would you like to get tea?"

Thea smiled. "I would like nothing more."

IN THEORY, IT WOULD HAVE MADE SENSE TO GET TEA AT THE cafe at Fletcher's. But they wouldn't be able to talk freely there. Or at least not as freely as they could at Claridge's tea room.

Stella had always spoken highly of it. When Thea was a girl, she found it to be loud and bright and too many people. After she came of age, she wanted to be around people even less. The sights and the sounds were overwhelming most of the time. Today, however, Claridge's became the perfect place to meet Leslie. It had the added bonus of being a perfectly acceptable place for a young, unmarried lady to meet an unmarried gentleman without a chaperone, though now that Molly's status as a married woman was known, she would have been a perfectly acceptable chaperone for such an adventure, had she not been part of the reason why they were meeting at Claridge's instead of at Fletcher's in the first place.

The tearoom was filled with fashionably dressed people and Thea could easily see why her fashion-obsessed cousin adored it so. Leslie met her there, having left Fletcher's first. In theory, they could have shared a car over, but Thea wanted to talk to Molly first so that she wouldn't be suspicious about Thea leaving.

"How is Mrs. Talbot doing?" he asked as she sat down across from him.

"She's shaken but trying not to show it."

Thea pulled off her gloves and tucked them under the napkin. She reached for the teapot and poured herself a cup.

"And you decided to investigate despite everything?"

Thea stared at her cup. "I didn't go alone."

Leslie let out a long-suffering sigh. "Because that makes such a difference." She glanced up at him. "Your maid or Mr. Poyntz?"

"My maid."

He closed his eyes and looked very much like he was

getting ready to groan again. "Is your maid, by chance, trained for such adventures?"

"Not to the best of my knowledge, no."

"Thea," he said, his voice soft. "I just don't want to see you get hurt again."

She let out a breath. "I know."

His hand reached across the table, fingers meeting hers briefly. "I don't want to step into Inspector Haddington's investigation. He's good at his job, but if it's all right with him, I'll help you look into this too."

"If they hadn't been threatening Molly, I wouldn't."

"We don't even know that it's the same person who killed Mr. Turner."

She glanced at their fingers and wished it would be all right to hold his hand properly. But for now, this would have to be enough.

"We don't," she agreed. "But does that really make it any better? There's a murderer running around as well as someone threatening Molly."

"We should still treat them as separate incidents until proven otherwise."

Thea sighed, but nodded. She wanted to find the person who was causing so much misery.

———

Upon returning home after leaving Claridge's, Thea knew she would need to find out who had an actual motive for hurting Molly if she wanted to contribute at all. The thought of Mr. Turner's ghost also lurking around the store was a problem. She didn't believe in ghosts, but Bridget did. If she mentioned seeing someone that looked like Mr. Turner without a logical explanation as to how she had seen him, Bridget wouldn't set foot in the store again.

Thea had no sooner reached the front steps leading up to the door than a cab pulled up to the curb.

"Greetings!" Wilhelmina Livingston declared as she stepped out of the taxi.

Thea blinked. In none of her letters had she known that Wilhelmina would be dropping by. She hadn't even known that she was back in London. Her last letter talked about the possibility of traveling to the Continent, to get away from the gossip for a while.

"Hello, Thea!" She leaned in and gave her a kiss on her cheek. "Did you miss me?"

"I did," she said, even as she watched her friend with complete confusion. "But I thought you were going to Paris."

Wilhelmina scoffed. "Paris is vastly overrated in autumn. Besides, James wrote me."

Another blink. "I didn't know the two of you kept in touch."

She smiled brightly. "Of course. How else would I hear what kind of trouble you've gotten yourself into? You certainly don't let anything slip in your letters."

"There's nothing to tell."

Wilhelmina laughed. "So there wasn't a body in Mrs. Talbot's store? You aren't investigating it? Mrs. Talbot isn't being threatened?"

Thea sighed. She supposed more help wasn't so bad of a thing. Still, she kind of missed the quiet days of only reading about murders. Wilhelmina linked her arm with Thea and they went up the stairs.

———

It turned out that her mother had invited Wilhelmina to stay with them at Prescott House. If the invite hadn't been sent before Thea returned home, she would have suspected that her mother was deliberately trying to make sure they always had someone with them. She would have suspected she was trying to avoid the subject of James, because while she agreed to have James over for dinner, every time Thea tried to ask about it, her mother suddenly had other plans.

"So, where are you staying?" Thea asked Wilhelmina. "After the trial, I mean?"

"I'm not sure yet. I'll have to start looking for somewhere. Perhaps a small flat. I don't need much space."

"You can stay with us," her mother said. "For as long as you need."

Wilhelmina smiled at her. "Thank you so much. I'd really appreciate that."

"You won't move back into your house?" Thea asked, brow furrowed.

"I'm not sure. I suppose it'll depend on if his parents allow it." She sighed. "I doubt they will, though. They were never especially pleased that I didn't give him an heir."

Thea listened to her mother make a noise of sympathy and understanding. "I can't imagine how difficult this whole situation must be."

Molly hadn't made it home for dinner that night. She telephoned earlier to let them know she would be late and Lionel said he would stay with her and see her home.

"It's definitely not something I thought would ever happen." She shifted, taking a bite and swallowing. "Whoever expects their husband to go blackmailing people? Or attempting to kill them?"

Thea's mother nodded sympathetically. "You've been through so much."

"I'm looking forward to some quiet." Thea didn't know how she knew, but somehow, she knew Wilhelmina was lying. But then, Wilhelmina turned to Thea. "What about you? Have you gotten involved in anything exciting since I last saw you?"

Thea swallowed and shook her head. She would never admit to her mother that she was looking into a murder. She could always tell Wilhelmina about the murder at Fletcher's later when they were alone.

THEA DIDN'T GET THE OPPORTUNITY TO TALK TO WILHELMINA before she retired for the night. Alone in her room, she sighed loudly. How did she keep getting into these situations? It wasn't like she went looking for murders and everyone kept telling her to keep away from it.

Mercury meowed loudly to let her know his demand to be picked up. She bent and gathered him into her arms. She petted his silky head. It didn't help as much as she hoped.

It was a bad pattern she needed to break. Thea felt like she was confident now, so why did she keep going back to the same old patterns of hiding away. She felt like she had broken out of her shell for the first time in years, but for some reason, being back at Prescott Hall made her feel small and insignificant. She felt like a child again, the same child who had left months ago. There was no reason, though.

"Are you all right, my lady?" Bridget asked as she walked into the room. The door squeaked shut behind her and Thea still felt the flutters of panic in her chest.

"No."

It was a more honest answer than she expected to give. Why was she not all right?

Bridget's steps came to a stop. "My lady? Is there something I can do to help?"

Thea shook her head. "I…" She never wanted to feel so weak and helpless as she did earlier. She turned and set Mercury down. "Can you show me how to open a locked door? Without a key?"

CHAPTER EIGHT

No one was downstairs when she went down for breakfast the next morning. It felt like a waste to have the table set for her, to be the only one there to be waited on. No wonder her mother disliked the formality of it so.

She wished she was a married woman, if only so she could take her breakfast in bed rather than come downstairs and be the center of attention. However, being alone did give her a chance to think and plan for the day.

She had glanced inside Mr. Turner's employee file the day before when she was in the offices at Fletcher's. She couldn't tell if he lived alone or with someone from the address, but she figured she would see when she got there. Mostly, she was surprised that he didn't live in one of the employee dormitories. She planned to have Bridget come with her and hoped that no one would wonder at two women going into a dead man's home.

Thea had picked out her plainest dark blue suit. She wanted to blend in and be completely unmemorable. It was one of her favorite suits for that reason, though Molly had often been annoyed that she wanted to blend in. Since discovering that Molly owned one of the most fashionable stores in London, it was really no wonder why she cared so much about the clothing.

Still, it would be best if she left before anyone saw her and asked any awkward questions. She planned to walk a few streets over and take a cab to the address rather than have Ezra take her and Bridget. The less anyone in the house knew, the less likely it was to get back to her mother about what she was doing.

Thea should have known she wouldn't be so lucky to leave the house without anyone spotting them, though.

"Off to detect?" Wilhelmina asked as she stood at the base of the stairs. She was dressed plainly as well, which seemed to fall into yet another persona that Wilhelmina had.

"How—?"

Wilhelmina smiled. "Mr. Poyntz told me."

Thea let out a groan. "Did he ask you to be my governess then?"

"He's right to be worried." Wilhelmina put her hat and gloves on. "The world is a dangerous place. And as much as you'd like to think otherwise, you're not really equipped to handle it."

Thea opened her mouth to protest, but what would be the point? Wilhelmina was right. James was right. It frustrated her dreadfully, but she wasn't as experienced in the world as they were. She was better off taking more than just Bridget with her.

"All right then."

Wilhelmina blinked and paused. She was clearly surprised at how quickly Thea acquiesced to her request. "Really?"

She nodded. "Yes. Let's go."

MR. TURNER LIVED IN A SURPRISINGLY BIG TERRACED HOUSE. Thea had assumed him to be a bachelor, so when she had given the address to the cab driver, she expected him to stop at something smaller. Perhaps a flat.

It looked like a family could live there. She hadn't seen anything in the file she took the address from that suggested he had a wife or children. But perhaps he did.

She looked at Bridget. It felt strange to break into someone's house if they were alive and living there. But Wilhelmina apparently didn't feel the same since she climbed out of the cab and marched up the stairs to the door. She knocked firmly, but no one answered.

Bridget followed her up the stairs. She opened the lock and they slipped inside before hopefully any of the neighbors could see them.

It felt odd to stand in a dead man's home. She knew it was her idea to go there but Thea had never actually been to someone's home to investigate a murder. Standing in the entrance hall, it was odd to see that the house wasn't dusty. Perhaps Mr. Turner had a maid who would clean and didn't know he was dead yet?

"Where should we start?" Wilhelmina asked her.

"We should look for the study." A house of this size had to have something. With any luck, Mr. Turner kept notes that would help explain why he, of all people, had been killed. From what Molly had told her, there was nothing particularly memorable about him, beyond the fact that he worked for one of the board members. Maybe he witnessed something or even had just been in the wrong place at the wrong time?

It took little effort to find the study. It was on the same floor as the entrance near the back of the house. Empty bookcases lined the one wall. Marks on the floor showed where furniture had once been. There was a desk near the center of the room, papers scattered across it.

Thea walked forward. There wasn't much of it that made sense to her at first. It just appeared to be dates and money. A ledger of sorts.

She sat down in the chair and tried the drawers. Only one was locked and she looked to Bridget again. Despite Bridget's lesson the night before, Thea was a long way from unlocking anything on her own. She only hoped that she would be more proficient at it before she really needed to know how to do it.

The drawer slid open and Bridget pulled out some papers. There was at least one blurry photograph, but one of the figures looked familiar. Thea was sure that she had seen the woman in the photo before. And the room they were in… it looked like the storeroom at Fletcher's.

"What is it? What did you find?" Wilhelmina asked as she stepped closer. The color drained from her face as she saw the photo and the ledger.

"It looks like blackmail." Thea set the photo down. The ledger had to be filled with payments. They didn't date very far back, starting only within the last year.

It was strange that the police hadn't visited his house yet and found these. It wasn't like she could take them and turn them in. After all, they would have to admit that they had broken into Mr. Turner's house.

"My lady, look at this." Bridget had picked up a framed photograph, one of the few trinkets she had seen.

In the photo, there was a young Mr. Turner with his parents. In fact, there were two young Mr. Turners with their parents.

It seemed that Mr. Turner had a brother, and they looked alike. Perhaps even twins. Thea let out a breath of relief. That explained the ghost she had seen. She knew ghosts weren't real.

CHAPTER NINE

THEA WASN'T GOING TO STOP BY FLETCHER'S THE NEXT DAY IF
it hadn't been for her mother asking her to pick out a gift for
Ilene, Thea's brother Cecil's wife and her former friend. Since
her brother and Ilene had gotten married, her mother had
picked out the gifts for Ilene's birthday. She supposed her
mother was bound to eventually tire of the strained relationship, but Thea wished it hadn't been so soon.

When it became known that Thea would inheriting her
aunt's fortune, she received a number of requests from suitors.
This was not helped by Ilene, who had been so happy with
Cecil that she decided Thea also needed to be in a relationship
to be happy.

"You've been so upset about your father," her sister-in-law
said at the time. "You need a house of your own to look after."

The problem was that Thea did not want a house of her
own to look after. She wanted to have a life and adventures
before she got married. If she could have the adventures after
that, she would happily marry now. But the idea of someone
else controlling her aunt's money made her sick. The idea of
them using it to hold on to a crumbling estate that was

mismanaging money was in the front of her mind every time a man with a title spoke to her, especially the ones Ilene had introduced to her.

Ilene found great satisfaction in being a mother and a wife. Satisfaction that Thea felt like she would never feel. Every time she saw Ilene with Zoe, she didn't think she was even capable of feeling that way. Maybe someday, but not yet. She didn't feel ready yet, not mature enough, not strong enough.

But telling Ilene, that was a mistake. Some things should not be spoken, not even to family. Especially not to family. She should have known better than to expect Ilene to ever understand how she felt about it.

She was lucky that her mother had never pushed about her and Ilene's falling out. Luckier still, that her mother had never asked for her to marry, like many of the mothers of the girls she knew would have. At twenty-two, several of her supposed friends had this charming way of making her feel like she was a spinster, and she didn't talk to more than a few of them outside of normal social occasions.

Leslie was the first man she had even entertained the idea of marrying after her father and aunt died. He didn't seem like he was even interested in her money or the social events that would make such fortunes relevant.

She was actually on her way to see Leslie. Since they were meeting outside in the park, Thea had brought Mercury in his basket. As she got dressed that morning, he hung at her heels, curled up under her hat, and stayed closer to her than he had in a few days.

She still had no idea what she even wanted to get for Ilene. Perhaps something small, like a locket that she could keep Cecil and Zoe's photographs in. That would be a nice enough gift for her, though some part of Thea felt like giving her nothing at all.

Mercury meowed loudly.

"Yes, I know you don't want to be here." She gave a scratch behind his ears and he preened. "Just a short stop in the jewelry department and then we'll be off to the park to meet Leslie."

It was on the way to the jewelry department that Thea got distracted at the glove counter. Pretty embroidered silk gloves lined the countertop and she couldn't help but stop and stare at them.

"Would you like to try them on?"

Thea smiled. "Yes, please."

She pulled her gloves off and told the girl at the counter her size. The silk ones fit like a dream. "Would you like them on your account?"

"Yes. And I was wondering if you can direct me to the jewelry department."

She reached down to stroke Mercury's head, surprised that he was behaving so well around so many people. It had been a struggle to get him to behave at the train station.

But there was no kitten in her basket.

Her breath caught in her chest. Where could he have gone off to? He was so small. He could be anywhere. Someone could have stepped on him or let him out the door. He could have burrowed into the fabric or under a counter.

"Mercury?" she called, though she didn't want to yell too loudly and cause a scene. Why had she told Bridget she could stay home? Why had she not asked Wilhelmina if she would come with her?

Blood pounded in her ears, and she wondered if she would have an easier time looking for him if she was on the floor.

"Mercury?" she tried again.

A giggle caught her ears. She turned sharply and pushed through the thankfully thin crowds until she heard the sound again. A younger girl, probably only about ten years old, held a piece of ribbon out to the tiny black kitten. He swatted at it, chasing it about, and she laughed again.

"You're such a good kitty," the girl told him, reaching to stroke his head. Mercury meowed loudly, rubbing his cheek along her palm.

"There you are."

The girl looked up with wide eyes. "I'm sorry. He just ran up to me. Is he your cat, ma'am?"

Thea smiled. "Yes, he is."

The girl picked him up gently and held him out to her. Thea took the kitten from her and pet his head. He purred loudly as if he hadn't just run off and caused her so much panic.

"What's his name?" the girl asked, her eyes still on him.

"Mercury."

The girl grinned. "Hi, Mercury. I'm Audrey."

She smiled at the girl. "Thank you for finding him."

"You're welcome."

"Audrey! There you are." The young man sounded as relieved as Thea had upon finding Mercury. He turned to Thea. "I hope she wasn't bothering you or your cat."

"Not at all. In fact, she found him for me." She kept a firmer hold on Mercury, wondering how she could keep him in the basket and from running off? Perhaps some ribbons or something tied to the handle?

The young man smiled brightly. "I'm glad she was able to help you." He turned to Audrey. "Come along. We need to be going now."

"Yes, Rex." Audrey smiled at Mercury and waved. "Bye, Mercury."

"Bye, Audrey. It was nice to meet you."

She took Rex's hand, and they walked away. Thea looked back to Mercury, running her hand along his head. "You're quite a naughty little thing, you know."

He meowed loudly and purred as she tucked him into the basket again.

"Please stay there this time."

He curled up, looking as innocent as could be.

THE PARK WAS RATHER QUIET. THEA SUPPOSED IT WAS BECAUSE it was a weekday and it was an odd time of year. The Season had finished and most people had returned to their country homes. For a moment, she longed for the days when they would have returned to Astermore. They would go for Christmas, but it wasn't the same. She missed her bedroom there, missed riding through the open fields and walking through the quiet village.

But she loved London, despite the crowds and the noise, though she was alone here far less often. Going out to the park was a breath of fresh air, but she didn't go nearly enough.

She spotted Leslie across one of the patches of green. His hat caught the sun and his whole face seemed to light up as he saw her. He moved towards her quickly.

"Hello."

"Hello." She could feel her cheeks heating up and hoped that her hat shaded her face enough that he wouldn't be able to see. Why did he have such an effect on her?

"Did you run into trouble?"

Thea glanced down at the basket, which one of the shop-girls had helped her tie several ribbons around the opening so Mercury should hopefully not be able to escape again. Mercury was napping contently like he hadn't caused such a fuss, and it was hard to believe that only a few weeks ago, he had been happy to stay in her pocket. He was much too small to be running about. "You could say that."

Leslie chuckled as he followed her gaze. He motioned to the path. "Shall we?"

She nodded. The path was shady and the autumn air felt nice. She wished, for a second, that he would reach out and take her free hand. But he didn't. She wasn't sure why she thought he would.

"You've been investigating still," he said finally.

"I have."

"Are you at least being careful?" She nodded again, and he let out a breath of relief. "Well, that's something at least." He glanced in her direction. "Did you uncover anything?"

"Mr. Turner had a twin brother. They look alike. I saw him at the store."

Leslie's face furrowed. "You don't think his brother killed him, do you?"

"I…" She hadn't given much thought to that. "It's possible."

"But your instinct is no. Have you met the other Mr. Turner?" Thea shook her head. "Then I'll ask Inspector Haddington to talk to him. Maybe he has some insight about what his brother was involved in."

Thea looked away. "Blackmail." Leslie made a noise, soft like he hadn't quite heard what she said. "The other Mr. Turner was involved in blackmail."

"How exactly do you know this?"

"We went to his house."

"And when you say 'we'…?"

"Wilhelmina and Bridget and me."

He nodded as if he had expected that answer.

"If you are going to keep investigating murders, you should probably learn some self-defense. Mrs. Livingston too. Jujutsu has been… popular among many women."

She understood his hesitancy to say it. Jujutsu was popular

among suffragettes. Even her cousin Stella had begun to learn it before she started rejoining the marches and attending meetings a few months after her daughter Imogen was born. Having a daughter be born into the world with so few rights renewed her passion for women's right to the vote. At the time, Stella had tried to convince Thea to learn with her and Thea had refused. Now she wondered if she ought to have learned. If nothing else, it would have been useful with all the situations she kept finding herself in.

The fighting suffragettes probably were something of a nuisance to the police, which explained Leslie's hesitance in telling her that. She couldn't deny, though, that the idea of being able to defend herself was appealing. She had spent the last few months getting into dangerous situations. She didn't want to be in that position ever again.

"I'll look into learning that," she said.

They strolled along for a bit longer in comfortable silence. Thea didn't quite feel like bringing up their investigation again and ruining their walk. It wasn't long, though, before, across the way, she spotted a familiar hat. Thea squinted, trying to see them clearer.

"What is it?"

"I think that's Wilhelmina—Mrs. Livingston."

She had been wearing that hat, a green one, this morning when Thea last saw her. Beside Wilhelmina, there was a man that Thea suspected was James.

Leslie let out a laugh as they walked closer and the woman turned and started waving at them. "It does appear that way, doesn't it?"

"Well, this is a coincidence," Thea said as they came to a stop before Wilhelmina and James. If Wilhelmina hadn't left first, she would suspect that they were following her. Perhaps they were anyway. With everything that had gone on, it wouldn't be the strangest thing to happen.

Wilhelmina smiled and glanced quickly at James. "It's nearly lunchtime. Won't you join us?"

Thea looked at Leslie. She had been looking forward to spending some time alone with him. But on the other hand, if she went with James and Wilhelmina, they would talk about the case.

Leslie seemed to be able to read her indecision. "That sounds like a great idea." He gave her hand a squeeze and gave her a long look that she figured was supposed to mean something. "Where did you have in mind?"

CHAPTER TEN

_____

On the way to Claridge's, Thea had stopped briefly at her house to leave Mercury in Bridget's care, as well as to drop off Ilene's birthday present. She didn't want to risk losing it, not when the gift felt so perfect. With barely a step inside, she was back in the cab, and shortly thereafter, she and Wilhelmina arrived at Claridge's to meet James and Leslie, who had gone there directly in order to secure a table.

They didn't start any real conversation until after the waiter left. Thea assumed they didn't want to be overheard, so it was surprising that they would be talking in public about it.

Three sets of eyes looked at her expectantly. She sighed. "So, you know we went to Mr. Turner's house—"

"You did what?" James asked. She ignored him.

"—and we found his ledger of blackmail."

James leaned forward, his eyes filled with anger. "Who was 'we'?" Thea glanced at Wilhelmina for half a moment, but it was half a moment too much. James followed the movement. "I see."

She was amazed how much disappointment he packed into

the two words, and even more amazed how much he sounded like her mother.

"We were careful."

Wilhelmina glared at Thea. They had most certainly not been careful, but she didn't want James or Leslie to worry. They were as careful as they could be.

"Perhaps you should tell us why you went there."

Thea glanced down at the silverware, flipping the fork over. She took a breath. "I thought I might find something. I thought that perhaps whoever had attacked Molly killed Mr. Turner." Perhaps they weren't connected, though. Maybe she was thinking about this all wrong. When she first got home, Molly said that the accountant for Fletcher's had just died. The ledgers were in code, there had been pages missing…

Leslie touched her hand, his fingers barely brushing hers. "What is it?"

"Daniel hadn't been very involved in the finances before," she told the other three. "But when Molly found out she was expecting, he decided he would focus more on Fletcher's and step away completely from his father's firm. Which was his plan all along, but whoever did this didn't know that." She closed her eyes for a second.

Why had they been downstairs? Had Mr. Turner been searching for something? Or perhaps the killer had been searching and Mr. Turner walked in on him or her? But what would be hidden in the storeroom?

"The accountant, Mr. Bexley, was the only one beside Daniel who knew the code to read the ledger."

"I looked into Mr. Bexley's death." Leslie pulled a file from his coat pocket and set it on the table. "It was declared from natural causes, but there's enough ways that someone could kill a person and make it look natural. Poisons and such. I don't think that person was working with Mrs. Stanton Fletcher, however. Mr. Talbot's murder seemed to be something of a happy accident for the person who might have killed Mr. Bexley. Assuming, of course, that he was killed and it wasn't just a matter of coincidence."

"The timing is odd, though," James said as he flipped through the file. "You've got to admit that, Thayne."

"But there were pages missing. From the ledger. And the pages that decoded the ledger."

She could see in his face that Leslie understood. "The envelope Mrs. Talbot had… the one from the train." She nodded and he let out a breath. "I'll see if I can find out what happened to it."

James frowned. "You think this envelope had something worth killing over?"

"Daniel thought it did." She glanced around the restaurant and saw the waiter returning with their food. The others looked up and quieted.

After he set the food on the table, he smiled at them. "Can I get you anything else?"

Leslie shook his head. "No, thank you."

Thea watched the waiter until he left before she turned back to Leslie. "You brought the envelope back to London after Molly gave it to you."

"I did," he confirmed. "But it was evidence. I had to turn it in in order for us to arrest Mr. Fletcher."

Wilhelmina leaned in. "What exactly was in this envelope?"

"Most likely those were the missing pages from the ledger." Leslie cut his meat, but didn't take a bite. "I looked at them at the time. They were definitely incriminating. Someone was stealing money, but it wasn't clear who. At the time, Mr. Fletcher seemed to be the obvious choice. He had gambling debts that needed to be repaid."

But Mr. Fletcher had long since been cleared. So whatever

was in the missing pages, whatever they helped decipher in the ledger, was probably the key to finding who had attacked Molly.

CHAPTER ELEVEN

THEA RETURNED HOME THAT AFTERNOON WITH WILHELMINA. She hoped her mother didn't discover she was investigating a murder, especially not with how easily Leslie and James pulled the information from her. Her mother had never forbid her from doing anything, though the last few years had seen her mother become much more averse to taking risks.

"Thea?" her mother called from where she stood in the doorway. She wore a tea-gown, and Thea had forgotten it was her at-home day for receiving guests and visitors. Like many other Americans who married into the English aristocracy early on, Vivien Prescott-Pryce had a wide range of friends who lived in London and often came to call on her. Few had happy marriages, but it had always been something of a tradition in their family to marry for love. Happy marriages produced heirs, she had heard it said. And though only the first male son could inherit, more children meant a better chance of one living until adulthood. It meant that they could marry children into other families.

Which was why people kept expecting her to marry. To secure an alliance for the future. If people knew James was part of their family, they would expect him to marry as well. She doubted he would be amiable to that idea. Still, she decided, as she looked at her mother, that she was going to invite James to dinner the next time she saw him. He clearly wanted to know his birth family, and she wanted him to be able to finally meet their mother. In a way, it would give her a bit of closure and peace with her father's wishes.

Her mother smiled. "Did you have a nice day out?"

Thea nodded, playing with a loose thread on the cuff of her glove. "It was quite lovely."

Wilhelmina volunteered. "We ran into each other in the park and decided to go to lunch at Claridge's. I have always loved it there. Such a beautiful place."

Her mother smiled. "I agree."

Wilhelmina continued with the bright smile she had used on the train. "If you don't mind, though, it was unseasonably warm outside. I would love to go up to my room."

"Of course."

Thea nodded. "That sounds like a good idea. I would like a chance to relax before dinner."

She didn't really want to face her mother's knowing smile alone. Every letter and telephone call from Leslie left her mother with a look in her eyes that made Thea not want to think about the implications of it all.

She and Leslie had no real relationship. Several letters, a handful of telephone calls, and a couple of walks at Ravenholm hardly made for much of anything. He was too busy with his work and Thea had barely been home long enough to contemplate what she was even hoping for from this. Would he even want to develop a relationship, she couldn't help but wonder as she climbed the stairs and opened the door to her bedroom.

She didn't want to have her heart broken if he didn't want to have anything more than a friendship between them. She liked their friendship. It was comfortable and safe. She hadn't known him very long, so pursuing a romance seemed like a way to ruin what they had between them.

THE NEXT DAY, THEA, JAMES, AND WILHELMINA WENT TO THE Bexley's house to speak to Mr. Bexley's widow. Wilhelmina insisted on coming for propriety's sake. As a widow, though she would not wear black for her late husband, Wilhelmina was a socially appropriate chaperone for a young unmarried lady such as Thea. For Thea to go anywhere private with just James, since it was not known to society that he was her relative, would be rather damaging to her reputation. With Wilhelmina escorting them, it wasn't nearly as scandalous.

Despite not being police, they could at least offer their condolences and see if Mrs. Bexley would be willing to part with any of her late husband's work. That was, of course, assuming he brought it home. If he was anything like Molly or James, he would have brought something.

But it had been over a month since he died. It was possible she didn't even have anything still.

When Thea's father died, her mother was quick to donate his clothes and give any of the books on the estate business to Cecil and the estate manager. His presence from Prescott House had been nearly purged overnight. The study there had been redecorated. Though, perhaps not everyone was so quick to try to move on.

They knocked on the door and a maid let them in, leading them to the drawing-room where Mrs. Bexley was receiving visitors. She was dressed in all black and was younger than Thea had expected from Molly's descriptions of Mr. Bexley.

Thea's brow furrowed. From the side, where the woman was nodding empathetically to an older woman who sat across from her at the table, she felt like she knew Mrs. Bexley. There was something oddly familiar about both of them, though she couldn't place it until the woman, seeing them out of the corner of her eye, stood to greet them.

"Louise?" Thea blinked as she recognized her old friend from finishing school. Thea, Louise, and Ilene had been close before Ilene became Thea's sister-in-law. After they finished school, Louise had disappeared into society, traveling to Paris for a time not long after that. They had lost touch, something Thea always regretted.

"Lady Theodora," Mrs. Radcliff, Louise's mother, said stiffly. Mrs. Radcliff was another reason why they lost touch. She had never passed along any of Thea's letters, as far as she could tell. Since Cecil had chosen Ilene over Louise, Mrs. Radcliff somehow found Thea responsible for it.

"I hadn't realized you married Mr. Bexley." Thea paused, wringing the handle of her purse between her hands. "My condolences on your loss."

"Thank you." Louise blinked. "I didn't know you knew my husband."

She glanced at her mother, who let out a long-suffering sigh. "Pardon me. I have another engagement. Louise. Lady Theodora." She nodded to James and Wilhelmina.

Thea bit her tongue. "A pleasure to see you again, Mrs. Radcliff."

Mrs. Radcliff left the room and Thea couldn't have been more grateful that she was gone. As if she would have had any say over who her brother chose to marry.

"Louise, these are my friends, Mrs. Wilhelmina Livingston and Mr. James Poyntz." She glanced back at James and Wilhelmina. "This is Mrs. Louise Bexley, formerly Miss Louise Radcliff. We went to school together."

Louise motioned to the chairs surrounding a table with tea. "Please."

They all took a seat and Louise served them. "I never actually met your husband. He worked for the husband of a friend of mine, Molly Talbot."

Louise let out a noise of understanding. "Mrs. Talbot has been very kind. She's visited a few times, but I understand she's quite busy, what with taking care of the store in her condition."

Thea wanted to laugh a little at the idea of Molly being in any sort of "condition". As if expecting a child would slow Molly down. She was rather a force of nature when she set her mind to it.

Louise straightened as she set the teapot down. "So, to what do I owe the pleasure? It's been quite some time."

Regardless of whether Mrs. Radcliff had diverted Thea's letters to Louise, Louise had Thea's address and could have written to her. But she had never heard from Louise, had no invite to her wedding, which had taken place not long after they lost touch, from what Thea had read in Mr. Bexley's employee file, perhaps only a month or so after Louise had returned from Paris.

Still, Thea forced a pleasant smile on her face. "It has been."

"Mrs. Bexley," James said, leaning in and giving her his charming grin. "I'm a reporter from the West End Gazette." Louise's brow furrowed, but James continued on, undeterred. "I know it may sound a bit unorthodox, but I am working on a piece about the people behind Fletcher's success. One of the names that came up was your husband's. Would you mind if I asked you a few questions about him?" His grin softened into something more genuine. "I understand it might bring up some painful memories you might not wish to talk about right now, but I would be ever so grateful for your time."

"You want to feature Mr. Bexley in your story?" Her forehead crinkled. "He was just an accountant."

James shook his head, opening a small notebook that Thea

recognized from when he interviewed her on the train. "Mr. Fletcher said that 'without Peter's contributions, we wouldn't have lasted a year.' And when I asked him to clarify, he mentioned that Peter was Mr. Bexley." He leaned in closer, like he was about to tell her some big secret. Louise mimicked his movement. She wasn't sure if it was subconscious or not, but a glance at Wilhelmina told her that she had spotted it as well. "I wonder if you might have heard about Mr. Fletcher's gambling problem—" The story detailing it had been in nearly every paper in London about a month ago, after Lionel was arrested. A prominent businessman arrested for the murder of his business partner was a big story, even if it was later proved wrong. And Molly and Lionel had worked to use that press in their favor. "—and Mr. Talbot was said not to have been as involved in the business."

Louise frowned. "Really?"

"That's surprising to you?"

"A little, I suppose. Mr. Talbot frequently visited after business hours the last few months before…."

"Do you know what about?"

She shook her head. "He and my husband liked to seclude themselves in the study for hours. He would arrive just after dinner and stay until nearly midnight. Not every night." She hesitated.

"What is it?"

"He—Mr. Talbot, that is—was here in the morning when I woke up on the day that my husband died." She blinked and shook her head. "He came the night before. I never heard him leave. And I never heard Peter come upstairs." She looked at James. "You don't think that they discovered something that was the reason that Mr. Talbot died, do you?"

Wilhelmina placed a comforting hand on the woman's arm. "The police confirmed that Mr. Fletcher's wife killed Mr.

Talbot for her own reasons, unrelated to anything that Mr. Talbot and your husband might have uncovered."

Louise let out a breath. "That's a relief, at least."

Thea shifted slightly in her seat. The whole situation felt beyond uncomfortable, and she was more than happy to let James and Wilhelmina lead the conversation. Never could she have anticipated that Mr. Bexley's widow would be someone she knew. Out of all of the people in England, it seemed like such a slim chance, so much of a coincidence that it had to be nearly impossible.

Fingers met her arm and squeezed ever so slightly before he withdrew. She glanced at James and smiled slightly.

He turned back to Louise and smiled charmingly again, and it was almost eerie as she could see her mother in that expression. "I was wondering if you might have anything of his? Journals or such that I would be able to look through?"

Louise nodded, eyes a little glassy. "Of course. I have everything still in the study. If you don't mind following me…."

CHAPTER TWELVE

"Well, that went rather well, don't you think?" Wilhelmina asked as they stepped outside onto the pavement into the sunshine.

"We have the cyphers," Thea said in disbelief. "We were so sure that someone killed him and yet they left the cyphers."

"We don't know that someone killed him," Wilhelmina pointed out.

"They didn't necessarily kill him at his home either. There's many ways to kill someone on a delay."

Thea tensed. She couldn't believe she had forgotten about the letter Bridget had found or their suspicions about James. But that sounded like an admission.

No, she told herself, there's plenty of reasons why he might know something like that. He's a writer, after all. Perhaps one of the stories he covered had been about poisons or something like that.

"Well, in any case, my vote is that we take this to Inspector Thayne before Thea manages to put herself in more danger."

"That sounds like an excellent idea," Wilhelmina teased as they climbed into the car.

New Scotland Yard was an impressive set of buildings along the Victoria Embankment overlooking the Thames. Thea never had reason to visit the Metropolitan Police's Headquarters before, but she had walked past the buildings when she went to the gardens near there. It had been years, though, and she really had no reason to pay attention to the buildings before.

"Lady Theodora?" a voice asked, and Thea turned to see where it had come from. Inspector Haddington stepped up to them. "Is there something I can help you with?"

"We were just stopping by to see Inspector Thayne."

The man nodded. "He was getting ready to leave right before I came down here. He should be here shortly."

Sure enough, a few minutes later, Leslie stepped out of the lift and walked through the atrium. His brow furrowed upon seeing them, but he didn't pause as he continued to walk towards them.

"We found something," she told him, holding out the leather-bound journal that was filled with the cyphers. "Did you find the missing pages?"

He nodded. "I did. But they're still in evidence."

Thea found the urge to sigh. She was curious to know what secrets they contained that Daniel would go through so much trouble to try to conceal them and that it was possible that Mr. Bexley had been killed for.

"I understand." She glanced back to where James and Wilhelmina were patiently waiting. She looked back at Leslie. "I should get going. It's getting late."

He nodded, his movements hesitant. "Of course. I'll let you know what I find out."

"That would be wonderful."

She hated how hard it felt to walk away. She gripped the

handle of her purse tighter. Why did it feel that way? She shook it off, careful not to let it show on her face. She rejoined James and Wilhelmina and they walked outside, back to the car where Ezra was waiting for them. She and Wilhelmina climbed inside and James waved them off.

THEA LIKED SITTING IN THE CAFE AT FLETCHER'S. IT WAS QUIET and allowed her a proper chance to think. Since she had been back in London, the house had seemed too loud, in a way that had nothing to do with their new permanent house guest or the kitten who'd taken up residence, sunning himself on her desk. She brought her notebook to the cafe, wanting to write down what progress they had made before she forgot.

When she reached the part about Louise, she froze, her hand trembling a little. She wished there was a way to bridge the gap between them, but there was no use in wondering what could have been, not after so much time had gone by. They were hardly the same people they were before they lost touch. It had been ages since she last spoke to her, a proper conversation and not just the pleasantries and interrogation of the day before. She had so many questions for her. Had Louise enjoyed traveling in Europe by herself? How had she met Mr. Bexley? What did she plan to do now? But she would never ask, not with the history between them. Still, it made her heart ache when she thought about what she, Louise, and Ilene once shared and how they would never regain that again.

She squeezed her eyes shut as the tears started to sting. She refused to cry over someone who discarded her so easily just because the memories had been drudged up again. Clearly, whatever they shared meant more to Thea than it had to Louise. It didn't stop the pain, though.

"Mind if I join you?" a soft voice whispered through the darkness.

Thea opened her eyes, blinking against the light. James hovered near the chair across from her, his face full of worry.

"You don't have to say 'yes' if you'd rather be alone. It's just, you don't look like you should be alone right now."

Thea let out a bitter laugh. "Is it that obvious?"

How stupid was she to let herself wallow in self-pity in public? People talked.

She motioned to the other chair. "Please, sit."

He slid into the chair nearly silently, effortless and graceful in a way that she was not but had always wanted to be.

"You're writing?" he asked, motioning to the journal.

She nodded. "Just trying to organize my thoughts."

Most of it was rambling, nothing worth much of anything. That journal told the story of a sad, lonely girl desperately wanting to fit in while wanting nothing more than to be left to her own devices.

James played with the silverware already on the table, twisting the napkin between his fingers. A nervous habit. Something that she would do.

"There's something I wanted to ask you about." The words fell from her lips before she could give them too much thought. If she thought it over too much, she would never ask him.

He hummed, the only indication that he had heard her.

She took a breath and spoke.

"I saw the blackmail letter."

She wasn't sure what possessed her to say, but from the way he jerked his head up to look at her, she was glad that she asked.

"What? When?"

"Before you left Ravenholm." She let out a breath. "I had Bridget search your room."

He stilled before his fingers ran through his hair. "I thought I lost that."

"It's an oddly specific thing to blackmail someone with."

He let out a sigh. "I do war correspondence. Well, general stories on wars in general, treaties, that sort of thing. Under another name. For another paper." His hands folded on the table, his knuckles turning nearly white from the pressure. "My uncle said no when I asked originally. Too dangerous, he said. But he can't stop me from writing for other papers. If I use another name, he can't track it too much."

"And the letter?"

"People hear spy and they get upset. Spies operate under a different set of rules than journalists. If people thought I was using my press credentials to go places, to gather information, doors would close." He shook his head. "Espionage is a little rich for my blood."

And yet, how was it really so much different than what they were already doing? Investigating murders when the police were supposed to be handling it seemed a bit like espionage.

"There was a photo of you in Paris with the letter."

He laughed. "A lot of news happens in Paris."

She felt almost foolish for believing the silly letter. After all, the younger Mr. Livingston proved he wasn't to be trusted long before he died.

"Were you going to pay him?"

Giving in to a blackmailer, especially when the information was false, seemed strange.

But James nodded, his expression solemn. "I didn't want rumors and lies getting out and doors to close to me. I like my job. But I also like when it goes smoothly." He sighed. "When I saw that Livingston had a similar letter to someone else in his room, I knew there was no point paying."

That made sense, in a strange sort of way. If someone was threatening her, who was to say that she wouldn't do the same.

James twisted the napkin in his hands again. "What happened to the letter?"

"I burnt it."

"Good."

"Why keep it? Why not burn it yourself, if you were worried about it getting out?"

"I was going to, but I didn't want to until after we found out who was doing the blackmailing, just in case. But then it disappeared." He glared at her but there was no real heat to it.

"And the guns? Being such a good shot?"

"My father took me hunting. Constantly. It was the only way he knew how to bond with me." He laughed, but there was very little humor in it. "I've been incredibly unlucky to be at the wrong place and the wrong time, or perhaps the right place at the right time, depending on how you look at it. But it's still enough to make everything seem suspicious."

"Coincidence can be a terrible thing."

He let out a bitter laugh and closed his eyes, running his hand through his hair again. "My life felt like it was being torn apart because of a stupid lie. I kept wondering 'who had found it?' and 'what would they do with it?' and waiting for the day I got a new blackmail letter."

Thea frowned. All of this could have been solved so easily had they just talked about it. A lot of things could be settled by talking. "Are you busy tonight?"

James blinked. "Not that I know of. Why?"

She pulled out one of her calling cards with her address on it, setting it on the table. "You're coming to dinner tonight."

His face went blank. "What?"

Thea fought the urge to sigh. "Mother and I are having dinner tonight while Wilhelmina is at another engagement. I want you to be there."

"Thea, no," he started to protest as she gathered her things and walked out of the cafe. James scrambled after her. "What if she doesn't want to see me?"

She stared at him. "You're being invited to dinner and that's the end of it. Dinner is at eight. Dress is informal."

CHAPTER THIRTEEN

Despite the fact that she told Mrs. Green that they would have a guest for dinner, Thea wasn't actually sure that James would show up. He might have decided it wasn't worth it. After all, it took him years to introduce himself to her. She wanted to think he would still show up, though. His curiosity should get the better of him and he would come.

Thea watched the street from her window. Not a car was in sight, not even a carriage or buggy. The lights were being lit slowly, drawing a pathway down the street. Mercury meowed loudly as he jumped onto her desk, just next to the window, and she scratched idly at his head.

"I know. I really thought he would come."

"My lady?" Bridget asked from the doorway.

Thea let out a sigh and turned away. Mercury cried out in protest but soon stopped when Bridget wrapped him up in one of the soft blankets and set him where he could watch over the street.

Thea walked down the stairs slowly, hoping with each second that passed that James would show up. She wanted

James and their mother to meet. She hoped that they might introduce him to Cecil and they could be a family.

A knock on the door startled her from her thoughts. Mr. Morgan walked quickly and opened the door. James stood there, the very picture of nervousness, and Thea let out a breath of relief. He stepped inside and Mr. Morgan closed the door behind James.

"I'm so glad you could make it."

James shuffled a bit awkwardly. "I almost didn't come."

She nodded. She suspected as much.

"Still, I'm glad you did." She motioned for him to follow her. They walked into the drawing-room where they would wait until Mr. Morgan told them to go through for dinner. Upon entering the room, her mother blinked, her eyes widening. Thea heard her breathe sharply.

"I hope you don't mind, but I invited James."

Her mother's eyes were fixated on James' face. He was watching her as well, a neutral expression fixed on his face. His hands tensed at his sides.

"It's very nice to meet you." His voice was nearly inaudible.

Her mother made a better effort at a smile. "It's nice to meet you as well."

The tension in the room was nearly tangible. Perhaps this hadn't been such a good idea after all. But she so wanted to have their family together. If an awkward, clumsy dinner was the price of that, then she was willing to pay that. So long as everything worked out in the end.

Mr. Morgan stood at the doorway. "I'm sorry to interrupt, my lady,"—not that anyone had been talking so much as staring—"but dinner is ready to be served."

They moved through to the dining room, which had been set with three place settings. Molly was resting. She had been tired when she returned from the store and asked that she not be disturbed. It was somewhat fortuitous, as Thea thought the stress from such an awkward dinner would put unnecessary pressure on Molly in her delicate state.

They took their seats and the food was brought in.

"So," her mother began, "Thea tells me that you're a journalist."

James shifted ever so slightly in his chair. "That's right."

"Do you enjoy it?"

James glanced at his plate before he nodded. "I do."

He looked back up at their mother, and for a moment, Thea wondered if it might be easier for them if she wasn't there for this. After all, they didn't really need an audience.

When they finished dinner, Thea excused herself under the guise of going to check on Molly. With a quick peek inside her door to confirm that Molly was indeed sleeping, or at least pretending to sleep, Thea headed back to her room. Mercury had crawled from his little blanket nest and decided he wanted to curl up by the fireplace instead. Upon hearing the door open, he lifted his head and meowed loudly.

"I suppose it's best to let them be. Don't you think so?"

Mercury let out a loud meow, licking his front paws rather delicately before he chased after Thea's shoe. He needed something better to play with than her clothing. She was fortunate that nothing had gone missing this time. After all, when he had taken to stealing her clothes at Ravenholm, Bridget thought that there was a ghost haunting them.

Thea sighed and picked him up, despite his loud yowls of protest, and walked over to her desk chair. She sat and tugged the curtain back slightly so she could watch down the street. No loud shouts or screams came from downstairs, so she took this as a good sign. Mercury squirmed, nudging his head until she climbed onto the desk and stared out the window as well, settling right on top of any papers she had foolishly left out.

He let out a soft sound and Thea ran her hand down his back until he was purring loudly, sounding rather like a car.

"You're talkative tonight, aren't you?"

Mercury turned his head, fixing his blue-green eyes on her. "Mrow?"

She resumed her petting. "I hope they'll talk. They are both important to me. I would like them to be in each other's lives. Perhaps it was selfish to force the issue. I'm not sure."

She petted Mercury's head one last time before she stood up and pulled the cord to let Bridget know she was ready for her.

CHAPTER FOURTEEN

Thea was in the storeroom of Fletcher's.

The sun shone brightly through the windows there that overlooked the delivery yard, but she wasn't able to see outside. No one was with her, which was odd, but she tried not to think about it too much.

Where were they, though? She couldn't remember anyone being with her. Had she come here alone?

The cat—the brown, black, and orange one who had been lurking in the storeroom when she was last there—sat in the middle of the floor, his tail swaying back and forth without a care in the world. Thea walked towards him and stooped down to his level.

"Did you have something to show me?"

He licked his paw and meowed loudly, walking towards the door again, the one where they had found the blood. He pawed at the door—hadn't there been crates in front of it? Where had they all gone?—and Thea pulled it open.

A noise behind her made her turn, seconds before she was pushed into the little room and the door bolted tight.

The room was small, so very small, and had it been that small when she was there with Bridget? She clawed at the handle, but it wouldn't open. She reached for the pins in her hair, but they fell to the floor and vanished. She banged on the door until her hands were bloodied, screaming until her voice was hoarse.

"It's no use," a man said in her ear. "They'll never find us here. You haven't found my murderer yet."

She turned, and seeing Mr. Turner as she had seen him that day watching her, she screamed.

THEA JOLTED UPRIGHT IN HER BED, PANTING HARD. THE ROOM was dark... too dark... and she stumbled out of the bed, despite Mercury's whine of protest, and stubbed her toe on the chair by the window as she felt to pull the curtains open. The light from the moon wasn't much, but it was enough to not be engulfed in the darkness any longer. With a bit of light, it was easier to breathe.

It was irrational, she knew, and yet, the dream haunted her. She wanted to find whoever killed Mr. Turner, but mostly so she could put her mind at rest.

Thea sat down on the edge of the bed and reached for Mercury. He cried loudly, letting his displeasure at being disturbed in the middle of the night be known.

"As if you don't usually wake me up," she murmured as she stroked his soft fur. Usually, he would walk across her at night and wake her from a sound sleep.

The fact that no one came running meant she clearly hadn't been screaming, and she was thankful for that small mercy. She would never hear the end of it if she had.

Thea turned and put her legs under the blankets, tucking Mercury in beside her. He shuffled and moved several times before he settled down, but his soft fur was comforting, ground-ing. The dream hadn't been real. Mr. Turner wasn't haunting her.

She whispered the words under her breath, over and over, until she fell back to sleep.

CHAPTER FIFTEEN

THEA CAME DOWN TO BREAKFAST THE NEXT MORNING TO FIND James at the table, eating breakfast while he read the newspaper and wearing the same clothes he wore last night. He didn't look overtired, though, and there were no bags below his eyes, so she assumed he must have slept somewhere last night.

"Good morning," Thea said as she paused in the doorway.

James looked up from his paper. "Good morning."

"Sleep well?"

"Quite." He looked back to his paper and wouldn't meet her eyes, though there was a slow smirk growing across his lips as if he knew what she wanted to ask but wouldn't.

Thea picked up a plate off of the sideboard and piled food onto her dish before she carried it over and sat down. "So, I take it your talk last night went well?"

"We have a long way to go, but yes, I think it went well."

"Good morning," Wilhelmina yawned. She usually took breakfast in bed, though she occasionally came down to eat in the mornings. It was always pleasant when she did, as Thea didn't particularly care for eating alone in the mornings.

Wilhelmina stopped short, rubbing her eyes, blinking several times. "Where did you come from this early?"

James folded the paper, looking at her. "I stayed here overnight."

"I see." Wilhelmina sat, pouring herself a cup of coffee and drinking it without adding anything as if that would help her. "Where did you sleep?"

James flushed. It appeared Wilhelmina had no qualms about asking such questions. "One of the bedrooms upstairs."

Wilhelmina raised her brow.

"Probably Cecil and Ilene's room," Thea said. For all of her mother's distaste of most traditions, she would never room an unmarried man on the same floor as three unmarried women, even if he was related to one of them and the other two were widows.

James blinked. Clearly, he had forgotten that he had more family through their mother than just Thea.

"Where will they stay then?"

James glared up at Wilhelmina. "I'm not moving here. I have my own flat." Wilhelmina raised her brow. "It was late when we finished talking, and she asked me to stay. It would have been near impossible to get a cab at that time of night."

Wilhelmina laughed. "I know. I heard you two talking when I came in."

It was nice to watch them talk like this. Wilhelmina often seemed a bit lonely, despite the fact that she had society friends. From Thea's understanding of them, they thought that Mr. Livingston had been a good husband and an excellent match for Wilhelmina. She wondered how often Wilhelmina pretended to be someone else for these friends and thought it had to be incredibly isolating to not be able to be yourself around others.

Thea finished her food. She smiled as she stood, glad that

Wilhelmina and James, two such important people in her life, could be friends.

———————

Thea returned to Fletcher's that afternoon without telling anyone. She wore her plainest suit and borrowed one of Molly's much plainer hats, and went without Bridget or Wilhelmina. She wanted another chance to look around, perhaps to find Mr. Turner's twin, without anyone looking over her shoulder or telling her it was too dangerous. She needed to go for her own peace of mind. After the dream last night, she couldn't get it out of her head. What if they had missed something? What if the other Mr. Turner knew something that could be helpful. She owed it to herself to go look.

If she had told Wilhelmina or James or Bridget about the dream, they wouldn't have let her go. Wilhelmina and James would have said it was affecting her and she needed to take a step back and be safe. Bridget would have panicked at the thought of a spirit haunting her from beyond. But the result would have been the same. She wouldn't be able to set foot in that storeroom to look around again if she had breathed a word of it.

The storeroom was like she remembered. The crates that blocked the door were near the wall instead, although one was now missing. She imagined it had inventory that needed to be unpacked and brought upstairs.

The cat from the last time was missing, surprisingly. Thea thought he might have lived there. Had he escaped somehow?

"There's a good kitty," a soft voice came from behind some shelves.

"Mrow."

"That's right. Eat your fill."

Thea rounded the corner. The man who had been feeding

the patched cat jumped, falling backwards until he looked up at her with Mr. Turner's face.

His clothes marked him clearly as one of the men who worked in the loading yard. It was perfectly reasonable for him to be there.

"I'm sorry, miss. I didn't know anyone—"

She shook her head. "It's quite all right." Thea smiled. "I was actually hoping that I would find you."

He blinked and she offered him a hand to steady himself as he stood. "You were looking for me, miss?"

"I was with Mr. Fletcher when we found your brother."

He inhaled sharply. "I see."

"I know it must sound awful, but I was hoping you might know something about what happened."

He shook his head quickly, in a way that it was obvious that he was lying. "I know nothing."

Thea took a step forward. "Whatever you say will stay between us. I just... I need to know why someone would kill him."

The other Mr. Turner scowled. His eyes darted back and forth. No one was down there with them.

And wasn't that the strangest bit? It was the storeroom of a busy department store. Where was everyone? How did they know to stay away?

Her voice dropped lower. "I know about the blackmail." He swallowed. "I don't know who he was blackmailing though." Mr. Turner glanced away. "Was it someone who works here?"

Slowly but surely, he looked back at her and nodded. She let out a breath and watched as Mr. Turner licked his lips.

"I'm not sure who he was blackmailing either, but—" He glanced around frantically again as if he was afraid he would be overheard. "I think they were someone important."

She frowned. That wasn't incredibly helpful. But still, if it had been someone powerful in Fletcher's who killed him, perhaps it did narrow the suspect pool considerably.

"Was it whoever he worked for on the board, do you think?"

Mr. Turner shook his head. "Mr. Hervey didn't like Mrs. Talbot. Charles, my brother, he said it often enough. He thought she should step down. But that's not worth killing over."

Thea agreed. Whatever Mr. Turner had been blackmailing the person with, it was far worse than something that was rather an open secret.

"How did you wind up in the docks and him for the board?"

It was rather strange, considering they lived in a middle-class home, albeit a rundown home, but still not the usual sort for manual labor.

"Charles and I were both working down here. Trying to keep the house when our mum got sick, you see. But he, I think he might have seen something, one of the nights he was working because one day I came in and he had been promoted."

Thea rather thought it sounded like he had blackmailed someone to get a better job. She supposed it made sense. People seemed to be capable of anything, if they were desperate enough.

"Do you know why it's so empty in here?"

He nodded. "We got told we weren't supposed to linger in here. It was a few days… before… but no one wants to hang around. Just in case it was random." He looked down at the cat that was happily lapping up the cream Mr. Turner had poured out for him. "I just came to feed him. He didn't deserve to go hungry, just because no one wants to be in here too long. It's not right."

She nodded.

"Is that all, miss? Might I go now?"

Thea nodded. "Thank you. You've been most helpful." She smiled sadly. "I'm sorry about your loss."

He bowed his head and left quickly through a side door that she hadn't remembered seeing before. Could whoever killed the other Mr. Turner that day have escaped through the door?

Thea walked forward and peeked out the window there. No. She didn't think so. The yard outside was quite busy. Someone covered in blood would have been rather noticeable. They had to have left the storehouse in another way.

She just had to figure out how.

Making her way to the little room again, just to reassure herself there was nothing else in there, she kept an eye out for people behind her. She didn't want to be pushed in like she had been in the dream.

She glanced back, then opened the door. The blood was merely a stain now. The signs that he had been in here were all but gone. If she didn't know better, she would have thought something had rusted on the floor, discoloring it.

Thea stepped inside the little room, looking around. Surely, there had to be something, anything that the police had missed. Why would her mind have fixated on this particular spot if there wasn't? She started checking the shelves one by one. Perhaps the police hadn't searched there. After all, this room was smaller than the main storeroom and out of the way. No one had disturbed it for days with the crates in front of it, so perhaps no one went in there regularly.

It was the perfect sort of place to meet the person you were blackmailing if they knew your identity. And whoever it was had to know Mr. Turner's identity since they were most likely the one to get him the job as the secretary for the board.

She paused. Perhaps it was Mr. Hervey. Mr. Turner worked for him as his secretary. He would know his secrets, but that didn't add up. He would have needed to know his secrets before in order to blackmail him into getting the job, and why come all the way down to the storeroom to meet someone you could reasonably meet in your office?

No… it made far more sense for it to be someone else on the board. They would have the means to pull the strings to get him hired, and meeting with him in their office too frequently would be suspicious without him having a legitimate reason to be there.

As she moved to leave, something caught her eye. It looked lighter than merchandise above it, and she supposed someone would have noticed it eventually. She reached up, awkwardly pulling at the unknown item while simultaneously trying not to drop the merchandise on her head. Finally, with a hearty tug, it came free.

Thea's brow furrowed. It was a small bundle of photographs wrapped in twine. A man and a woman caught in a rather indecent manner. Though both were fully clothed, there was little doubt about what they could be doing. The man's back was to the camera in the first picture, but the woman's face was quite clear. Thea didn't think she could ever forget it, not when the woman in it had tried to kill her on a moving train. To see Mrs. Fletcher left her stomach twisting into knots.

In the next photo, Mrs. Fletcher had straightened up. The man was fixing his clothes—thankfully—and they must have heard something because the second photo held a much clearer shot of his face. She didn't recognize him, but it certainly wasn't Mr. Fletcher. It wasn't Mr. Turner either, which lent further credence to her theory that he was black-mailing whoever the man in the photos was.

Thea breathed in shakily. No wonder someone would be willing to kill to keep this a secret. She wondered if Lionel knew.

Somehow, she doubted it. If he had, she thought that the police might have known about it. She would have to ask Leslie, but first, she needed to get out of there without anyone seeing the photos. She didn't want to be in danger if the wrong someone saw her with them.

She worked the photos between her corset and chemise, buttoning her shirt back up and making sure as best as she could that not a hair was out of place before she left the little room.

Maybe the negatives were still at his house. That would most likely prove that the photos were his.

Thea walked quickly across the storeroom. She wanted to get out of there as fast as possible before anyone had questions about what she was doing there.

She was up several stairs when the patched cat let out a howl like she had never heard. Thea turned on the stairs, looking down at him for a moment, as a shadow came up behind her. She turned as the shadow shoved her hard. A sharp crack echoed in her head, and the world went dark, the smell of something citrus in the air.

CHAPTER SIXTEEN

THEA SAT UP, HER HEAD ACHING. SHE BLINKED AGAINST THE light. The sun was far too bright and she squinted as she pushed herself to her feet.

The floor swayed beneath her and each step was like walking on a boat on a rocky sea. She reached for the wall, the only thing steadying her as she took each stair carefully.

"Oh my!" a young woman in a black gown gasped as she came down the stairs. "Miss? Are you all right?"

That seemed like a rather silly question. She felt awful and she imagined she had to be a sight.

"I need to get upstairs." If she could get upstairs, she could telephone the police.

The young woman watched her skeptically. Still, she raced forward and offered an arm, keeping her steady as they walked slowly up the steps.

"Only a few more to go."

Thea gripped the young woman's arm tighter as her vision started to spot. She was thankful when the next step she took forward was at the same height as the one before. She stumbled a bit, and the woman grabbed at her arm, holding her upright.

"Can you take me to the telephone?"

The woman frowned, but they began walking again. It wasn't long before they reached a phone in one of the offices, and the woman helped Thea into a chair. A secretary at a type-writer stood up, a question on her lips.

"Will you call the police, please?" The secretary nodded, moving to the phone and picking up the receiver as she held it to her ear. Her lips seemed to move and she said something, but Thea couldn't hear her. The young woman who found her shook her arm, a bit frantic, but Thea felt so tired. Her eyelids were so heavy. She would just close them for a moment or two. Just until the secretary had finished on the phone.

CHAPTER SEVENTEEN

"WELL," WAS THE FIRST THING THEA HEARD WHEN SHE WOKE up again. "You gave us all quite a scare."

The words seemed like a joke to be thrown out carelessly, but the manner in which they were spoken fell flat of that.

"James?" The name sat heavily on her tongue and it felt like she was trying to speak through molasses or honey. She tried to sit but gentle hands pushed her back down. Something cold on her head shifted, but one of the hands moved from her shoulder to move it back to the spot that was sore on her head. "Where am I?"

"In the hospital," a different voice came. Thea blinked her eyes open and found the hands on her shoulders were Wilhelmina's.

At the foot of the bed, Leslie stood. It was rather inappropriate, two men visiting her in the hospital. Still, the sight of his concern warmed her heart.

"We told them we were family," Wilhelmina whispered. She motioned at James, then Leslie. "Your brother and cousin, and I'm your sister-in-law."

She laughed but it hurt to move her head.

"Do you know what happened?" Leslie's face was serious, holding none of the joking manner that Wilhelmina did.

Her brow furrowed as she tried to remember. "I was pushed." Her eyes widened. "I was wearing Molly's hat."

"What?"

"Molly's been attacked a few times."

James groaned and Leslie pressed his fingers into his forehead. "What would possess you to wear her clothes?"

She grimaced. "I wanted to be unnoticeable." Wilhelmina frowned and Thea shifted. Beneath her corset she could feel the pictures still pressed to her skin. "It was worth it. I found something."

James' eyes narrowed. "Worth risking your life over?"

Perhaps not. She had been so stupid to go alone. It had been so foolish and now she would pay for it. Thea closed her eyes, letting the ice cool the soreness.

"I can show you." She shifted slightly in the bed as she opened her eyes. "However, you'll need to leave. I—um… I hid it."

James blinked and Leslie frowned before understanding seemed to dawn on him. "We'll be right outside. Let us know when to come back in."

Thea unbuttoned her shirt with some difficulty, once they were gone and the door was closed, and pulled the photos out. She let Wilhelmina help her button her shirt back and leaned back further against the pillow. Wilhelmina opened the door.

Thea offered the photos to Leslie, who took the small bundle with a frown that seemed to be permanent now. "I found them in the storeroom. They were hidden and…."

"Is that Mrs. Fletcher?" James asked as he peered over Leslie's shoulder. He tilted his head slightly, brow creasing. "The man, he looks familiar. I can't quite place him, though."

"I think he might be one of the board members at Fletcher's."

He nodded, but for some reason, he didn't look convinced. Perhaps it was just the head injury. "That must be it then."

"Do you think this was your attacker?" Leslie asked, holding the photos out to her so she could study them again.

Who had pushed her? It wasn't the man in the photos, she didn't think.

James moved closer. "Close your eyes." She did. "You're standing where?"

"On the stairs… the cat that was down there, it screamed."

The man in the photos was younger. The one that had pushed her had been shorter, older. His cologne, which she imagined the scent she smelt must have been, had been quite potent. She would know if she saw him again.

"Do you think you'd recognize your attacker?"

She nodded.

THEA WAS RELEASED FROM THE HOSPITAL THE SAME DAY, thankfully. Despite losing consciousness, the doctor didn't think the bump was that bad. She would need to rest for the next few days and James and Leslie both forbid her from doing anything reckless in the meantime.

Her mother stood in the entrance hall when they arrived back at Prescott House. Her face was full of concern and she reached for Thea, despite her being supported by Leslie and Wilhelmina.

"When Molly phoned and said you were taken to the hospital, I assumed the worst."

"It's nothing. I fell," she lied. "It's just a bump to my head."

"I was so worried.

"I'm all right. Honest. I think I could just use some rest."

Her mother looked at Leslie. "Is that true?"

He nodded. "It is."

Ezra stepped forward, offering his arm to Thea. She took it and let go of Leslie. She smiled at Leslie.

"Get some rest."

She nodded.

The stairs seemed like an impossible task. Still, with Wilhelmina and Ezra's help, they took each step slowly, one at a time until they reached the first floor, then the second. She cringed at the thought of going any further, but her bedroom was on the next floor, and she really would much rather rest in her own bed.

She also desperately wanted a bath. Though it wasn't a bad injury, there had still been blood, and she would much rather go to bed without the grime from the storeroom floor.

They reached the third floor and the three of them maneuvered through the narrow doorway so that she could sit.

"I'll send Bridget up, my lady," Ezra said before she could open her mouth. Thea nodded and watched as he left the room.

Wilhelmina watched her with a curious expression.

"What is it?"

"You should have told me where you were going." Her head tilted a little. "I'm not like Inspector Thayne. I wouldn't have stopped you. But going into a situation you knew could be potentially dangerous was stupid."

"I know."

"You could have been killed."

"I swear I hadn't planned on getting involved in a murder investigation." She glanced towards the doorway and hoped no one was on the other side listening. "I just wanted to help Molly." She didn't care about anything else. She just didn't want Molly to be in danger because someone had decided that they didn't like her being in charge of the store.

Bridget stepped inside and Wilhelmina nodded. "I'll let you rest."

IT WAS WITH GREAT EFFORT THAT BRIDGET HELPED THEA TO the bathroom once a hot bath was drawn. Getting undressed was a Herculean effort. Every inch of her body ached.

"My lady," Bridget grasped a bit more of the damage. Her back had to be bruised. Besides her head, it had taken quite a bit of an impact.

"Is it bad?"

Bridget loosened the laces on her corset and helped her take it off. The rest of her undergarments came next. Part of Thea wished there was a mirror in the bathroom. She wanted to know how much was bruised, but she also didn't want to know.

Thea needed Bridget's hands to steady her as she lowered herself into the tub. Her hands were beginning to shake with the stress of the day beginning to wear off. She was safe in the bath.

Mercury managed to press against the door, which hadn't been closed tightly, it seemed, until it opened. He stood in the doorway for several minutes, staring unblinkingly. Bridget turned and drew a sharp breath.

"I'm so sorry, my lady. I must not have closed the bedroom door all the way."

"That's all right." Thea pulled a wet hand from the tub as Mercury strode closer. Water dripped onto the floor, but he didn't seem to mind that her hand was a bit wet as he nudged his head under her palm. The soft fur was calming. She ran her hand down the length of his body, feeling him breathe gently under her fingers. "You just wanted to spend time with me, didn't you?"

"Meow."

She smiled as he purred loudly.

BEDREST WAS DREADFULLY BORING. THEA HATED NOT BEING allowed to get up or go anywhere, though she did have to admit, the rest did her good. Mercury seemed to enjoy it at least, alternating between laying on her legs and resting his head on her thigh so she could stroke his head. Not only that, it allowed her time to write her experiences in her journal. She wanted to make sure that she wrote down everything she could remember. Every detail, down to the most minuscule thing, found its way into the journal, until she suddenly ran out of space and had to send Bridget to the store to buy her another book to write in.

Beyond writing, Wilhelmina spent a fair amount of time in the room with her. When she was deemed well enough to go downstairs, the drawing-room became her new haunt. In the past, she never spent much time in the drawing-room. It was decorated to her mother's tastes, not Thea's, and she found the room to be a bit much. The curtains were a vibrant blue, the rug something more expensive than her wardrobe for the Season, and the couches all a swirling pattern. There was nothing wrong with it but it somehow used to make her feel like more of a child.

Supervised meetings in that room with potential suitors didn't help that. And there had been many who called the first year after she had been presented. One of the few British heiresses in her own right, Thea had become an attractive prospect for many of the men she met that year, although less desirable when they realized she had no interest in marrying and turning over her fortune to her husband. To her great relief, the next year, word seemed to have spread, and interest waned.

When she spent too much time thinking about it, the errant thought of "Would Leslie make her sign over her fortunes" would pass through her mind, and she would immediately have to scold herself for thinking such things. They had only known each other a few months, and while people certainly married in less time, it had never been Thea's way to jump with both feet without looking.

Not before the train anyway.

Wilhelmina was brilliant with numbers. When they got their hands on Fletcher's ledgers, a project that she suspected Leslie believed would keep Thea from wandering into trouble again, Wilhelmina had managed to find several spots in barely any time.

"My grandfather taught me." Wilhelmina shrugged. "He liked numbers. Grandmama thought it was silly that I wouldn't learn, especially with my stepmother's desire to bring me to England to marry. 'Budgeting for taking care of a house is like running a business,' Grandfather always said."

The numbers made little sense to her. She had never been quite as adept at math. The numbers gave her a headache, and with the head injury, it only seemed to be compounded.

Wilhelmina frowned.

"I think I might have found something." She stood, bringing the ledger from the store along with the book from Mr. Turner's home. "The dates that the inconsistencies are on coincide with the dates that Mr. Turner marked as getting paid."

"It's the same days?"

Wilhelmina shook her head. "A day or two before in most cases, but occasionally on the day of. But it's close enough."

"So whoever was stealing the money from the store was using it to pay Mr. Turner off?" She thought back to the pictures.

"Do you think that maybe we had this all wrong? Perhaps Mr. Fletcher knew about his wife's affair and was paying to keep it quiet?"

Thea shook her head. "Lionel was insistent that he didn't know. And I believe him."

She closed her eyes and thought back to the day in the cellar. The day she had found the body. Lionel had been with her the whole time. He wouldn't have been able to kill Mr. Turner and move him and find the body. He wouldn't have been so pale upon finding him. He had been genuinely surprised to find him there.

And if Lionel had known about the affair, why wouldn't he have told the police about it when he was being framed for Daniel's murder? Especially when it became clear that Mrs. Fletcher was the one framing him?

"I think Daniel and Mr. Bexley realized that it wasn't just someone stealing money. Wilhelmina flipped to the back of the book, where everything had been written upside down and in that strange code. "Look. Over here"—she pointed—"is where those pages that Inspector Thayne received from Molly go. And they pointed out the regularity of the payments, as well as the increases."

Thea frowned as she looked. She could barely make out what was written on those papers. The handwriting was much too small and cramped.

"I'll take your word for it." She sighed, leaning back against the couch, though her movements were still slowed. The bruising on her back, while it had gone down, hadn't healed completely yet. According to Bridget, it was all a sickly sort of yellow and purple where it began to fade. Perhaps going in without thinking things through really wasn't worth it.

Before, she had suffered injuries, but nothing like this. The others all healed quickly. This had been the gift that kept giving. At first, the headaches kept her awake at night. The lights were too bright. Everything was too loud. Then, when those started to subside, she was unable to lean against anything, not even the pillows. A corset was impossible, and she gave up quickly on that idea, despite the doctor telling her she was recovered.

It seemed that her corset protected her ribs and back from the worst of the fall that day, but in return, the boning left the long bruises across her back. A tea gown, with its lack of undergarments, was far more comfortable and more suitable for her state until she was able to dress properly and return to the rest of the world.

Although at the rate everything was healing, she might have a full novel of her exploits written. James found it amusing, at least, in the rare times he visited, which always seemed to coincide perfectly with when her mother left the house.

Artemis and Apollo, her mother's Blenheim Spaniels, did not like Mercury any more than he liked them, though. Sharp lines of territory were drawn in the house by them. As long as Mercury didn't go below the third floor—or if he did, it had to be in the servant's stairs—Thea never was startled by hisses and barks. The dogs never came farther up than her mother's rooms on the second floor, and for the most part, Mercury was more than happy to spend his time sunning in the nursery.

During her rest, she attempted to introduce them more than once, with varying degrees of success. Mercury did love to be the center of attention, though, and wasn't as gentle of her injuries as the dogs were. Despite being so small, she could feel every ounce of his weight when he flopped on top of her. The dogs, used to being firmly disciplined, were much better behaved when not provoked. They adored being petted on their silky ears, and even silkier fur, and Thea never felt like she was annoying them the way she sometimes felt with Mercury. There was also the fact that they didn't lay down on her journals when she was trying to write. This was, perhaps, the worst of Mercury's crimes. The more engaged she became with writing down the stories—and if she exaggerated or fabricated some of the details, who would really know—the more annoyed Mercury acted towards her.

As if he lacked attention. Bridget catered to his every whim. When she was unavailable, Thea caught Nellie sneaking away to fawn over him. And she knew he had managed to convince everyone below stairs that he was starving, crying loudly until he received extra bowls of cream and a helping of fish. She was impressed, since Mrs. Smith never gave her or Cecil extra food outside of meal times, not unless their parents requested it. They snuck into the kitchens so many times as children to try to steal biscuits. It was the few times Thea could convince Cecil to join her on an adventure. The promise of food always lured him, though these expeditions were never fruitful.

"I do believe you're correct. I think it has to be whoever the man in the photos is." Wilhelmina closed her eyes. "It's a shame that Inspector Haddington doesn't have enough evidence to convict him. Perhaps he didn't murder Mr. Turner, but shouldn't there be some record somewhere of who made these changes?"

Thea laughed. After days of going around in circles looking for some shred of proof, it wasn't the strangest thing that Wilhelmina had said.

She sat down in the chair across from the couch with a loud sigh.

"Perhaps let's take a break?" Thea suggested. Wilhelmina nodded, and Thea reached for the teapot to pour them both a cup. "What are your plans? After this is solved?"

Wilhelmina opened her eyes, a serious sort of expression crossing her face. "James mentioned something that caught my interest. Inspector Haddington, as well."

"Oh?"

"A woman can go places a man cannot. I'm thinking of

looking into the proper paperwork and necessary training to become a private detective."

"A real lady detective?"

Wilhelmina smiled.

"Seems like something from a penny novel, doesn't it?" She shook her head. "Inspector Haddington told me that Scotland Yard sometimes hires lady detectives. And James mentioned that women will often hire other women, especially to prove adultery." The smile fell from her face. "If I can help some other woman not go through what I did and help her secure a divorce, it would be worth it."

Thea nodded. "That makes sense." Her brow furrowed. "Will you stay here, though?"

"For as long as your mother and you will have me."

Thea could barely suppress a snort. "My mother adores you. She'll be happy to have you here for as long as you want." She couldn't suppress the smirk that overtook her face, not that she tried very hard. "And there's still a chance for you to become her favorite daughter-in-law."

It took a few seconds for her words to sink in and a flush to spread across Wilhelmina's cheeks. Still, she shook her head. "There's nothing between James and I. Not like that, anyway."

Thea fought a laugh. Both of them clearly had feelings for each other, though she supposed it was a bit like with her and Leslie. Wilhelmina only knew James a short time, and she had been married for most of that time. Society expected her to at least mourn for her husband, despite him being a criminal. It might have been easier for her, kinder even, if Mr. Livingston had sought a divorce before his death, since his parents took control of everything anyway. A divorced woman was expected to mourn for less time than a widow was.

"Maybe someday?"

Thea bit her tongue as the words came out and looked down

at her tea instead. Was she really suggesting that another friend marry her brother? But James was not Cecil, and Wilhelmina was far more mature than Ilene had been when she married Cecil. And unlike Ilene, Wilhelmina would respect her wishes, no matter what they were. The fact that she faced danger with her rather than pulling her away from it was proof of that.

MOLLY WAS AVOIDING HER. IT TOOK A NUMBER OF DAYS FOR Thea to realize this. The first few, she had been in her room and hadn't noticed. But when she was able to go downstairs, she noticed Molly hesitating in the doorway when she was in a room. Molly only would enter if there were other people as well, such as during dinner time. It seemed she needed a buffer in order to spend time with Thea, which hurt more than she could put into words.

Until the train, she thought they had been close friends. After all, she had been Thea's most trusted confidant and companion for years. Ever since then and the revelations that came with it, it felt like a sea too vast to cross formed between them. Thea was dealing with a different person with Mrs. Margaret Talbot than she had with Molly Forbes, a complete stranger who couldn't even tolerate talking to her alone.

"Molly?" she called when she saw her in the hallway, about to go upstairs.

Molly hesitated but didn't turn around.

"I…" She trailed off. How did she even start a conversation like this? Social interactions that included confrontation between people you didn't want to offend were still not her forte. She let out a breath. "You've been avoiding me."

Molly stiffened. "Have I?"

"Please… just look at me. Talk to me." Molly turned slowly,

though her gaze was over Thea's shoulder rather than her face. "Why have you been avoiding me?"

"I-I..." Her hands shook. "How do you think I felt when I saw you sitting there with all that blood?"

The words were spoken with a sharp bite, but underneath, there was real fear. She stalked forward, eyes a bit wild.

"I can't lose anyone else. And I saw the hat you were wearing. You were attacked because of me."

Thea took Molly's hands and squeezed them. "I'm sorry for worrying you."

"Please, just don't put yourself in more danger because of me. I don't think I could bear it."

Thea nodded. She couldn't promise that, but she would certainly try to be more careful in the future.

CHAPTER EIGHTEEN

THE SUN MADE FOR A BEAUTIFUL DAY, WITH JUST ENOUGH breeze in the air to be pleasant, and so Thea had opted to have Ezra drop her and Bridget off a few blocks from Fletcher's. She wanted to tip her head back and let the sun warm her face. The fresh air would do her good after being cooped up in the house for so many days. She didn't think she could have stood to be there another day.

The street was fortunately not too crowded, so no one bumped into them as they walked.

"Are you happy to be out again, my lady?"

"Immensely."

As they paused at the street corner, she did lift her face to the breeze, the sun kissing her cheeks. She tried to ignore the plethora of scents that wafted in their direction and just enjoy the wind against her skin. This was what she missed about the country when she was in the city. She wanted to be able to breathe clean, fresh air. Still, she wouldn't trade London for anything.

She lowered her face and they crossed the road.

For some reason, Thea expected Fletcher's to look different

now. Instead, the same doorman was at the door, letting people in and helping shoppers to their cars. The same displays were still present on the floor when she walked in. The same hats hung on the haberdashery counter. How strange of a feeling for everything to have changed so much for her and not the rest of the world.

Even the specials for the cafe were the same that day.

Thea found Leslie easily, exactly where he told her he would be when he called her the night before to make plans. They would be eating an early lunch before they tried to identify her attacker.

She didn't think the task would be too terribly hard. Though she didn't get the best view of the man who pushed her, she had smelt his cologne, which matched up to Molly's recollections of the man who had attacked her previously. She had never gotten a clear enough look at the person who attacked her, but paired with Thea's descriptions, Leslie and Constable Cooke thought they might be able to find the person who had been attacking Molly once and for all.

Leslie stood as he saw her. He smiled, eyes trailing over her before he nodded ever so slightly.

"You look well."

"Resting was good for me, I suppose."

He laughed a little at that.

It was true, though. She felt so much freer after writing down all of what had happened. Now that it was no longer living inside her head, she felt lighter than she had in ages. When was the last time she felt like this? Before her father died, perhaps? When her cares seemed so much less.

"I'm sorry for worrying you." They sat. "I realized how foolish I had been."

He smiled and she was struck with a sudden urge to reach across to him and a wish that he would kiss her hand again like he had at Ravenholm. But he would never touch her like that, not in public. It was too improper. Still, it didn't stop her from wishing.

"I'm not the only one you worried."

She sighed. "I know. James let me know, at length."

After all, James wrote for a living. He had no shortage of words to tell her exactly what he thought about her going off by herself.

The food came shortly after and then they were in the lift up to the offices. Most of the board members weren't usually there, but another session had been called, so all they had to do was wait for the meeting to let out. Since they suspected it might be one of the men or one of their assistants acting on their behalf, this would be the best way to allow Thea a good look at all of them without arousing their suspicions. With her and Molly's testimonies, the police would be able to arrest him on suspicion of attacking them. It was their hope that the man who did it would confess.

To help further throw off any suspicion, Thea wore one of her brighter suits. She bought it a few months ago on a whim, a dark magenta color that she never found an occasion to wear before.

Today she wanted to look as different from Molly as she could. Bridget styled her hair differently this morning than her usual style, and the hat she wore was far bigger than what she usually wore.

Wilhelmina walked over to them as they stood outside the doors where the meeting was taking place. She held a small book near her side, partially hidden in her skirts, walking quickly as if she didn't want to be noticed.

"I found something."

Leslie's brow furrowed.

"You found something?" His eyes narrowed. "Where?"

"One of the secretaries, one who isn't in the meeting. They told me that their boss has been acting suspiciously the last few weeks. I may have given him the impression that I was working for you and Inspector Haddington and he let me into the office to search."

Leslie pinched his nose.

She offered him the book. "The dates in his schedule match up to the dates in Mr. Turner's ledger." She reached into her pocket and held out a locket. "And there was this in one of the drawers."

Thea took the locket and pressed it open. A photo of Mrs. Fletcher was inside of it. A lock of hair was secured on the other side.

"I also found out that he was married. I do believe his wife will be interested in seeing those photos."

If someone wished to prove adultery in order to gain a divorce, there were few things clearer than photographic evidence of it.

"That wasn't even the best that I found."

Leslie eyed her warily. "I'm almost afraid to ask."

With her other hand, Wilhelmina held out a bloodied handkerchief. "He seemed to have panicked that day and has tried not to think about it since, because his clothes are still in the office as well."

"Which offices did you say these were in?"

Wilhelmina smirked. "Mr. Richard Selkirk."

It was, of course, at that moment that the doors swung open. The meeting clearly adjourned and people began to walk out. While the man who had attacked her didn't seem to be among them, as there was no one with a similar build to the man, the man from the photographs was there.

He was almost handsome, if one liked older men. She could see perhaps why Mrs. Fletcher decided to pursue him.

Leslie stepped up to him. Instantly, Mr. Selkirk stiffened.

"I'm arresting you on suspicion of the murder of Charles Turner."

"You can't do that."

"You do not have to say anything…."

His voice trailed off as they walked farther away.

Thea could feel a presence hovering by her shoulder. She glanced back at her brother.

"I interviewed him," James said with a frown. "A few days before the murder. My uncle asked me to do it. It was about another business he had been involved with. An investigative piece."

Thea blinked. "I didn't see it."

She had been trying to keep an eye out for James' work after his revelation.

"It never ran. But I have the story and the research from it." He shook his head. "I didn't even make the connection."

"Will you be giving it to the police?"

He nodded. "And perhaps my uncle will run it this time."

CHAPTER NINETEEN

After Mr. Selkirk's arrest, Thea, Wilhelmina, and James decided to go back downstairs. There was no reason to stay upstairs if the other board members and their staff had already left.

"I feel so helpless," Thea told them. "I wanted to be useful. I thought that I might be able to find something that would let me help Molly."

Instead, all she had done was stress Molly more. That couldn't be good for the baby.

She closed her eyes.

"Leslie mentioned that I should look into some jujutsu training." She would write to Stella and see if her cousin could recommend any teachers that would be willing to teach her.

She didn't want to be so defenseless again.

They walked into the cafe, despite that Thea had eaten not that long ago. The tables would be useful for James to sit and write some notes for his story, and it wouldn't draw nearly as much attention to them as if they were standing in the store. The cafe was still open to the store and they could still see the people who passed as they shopped.

"That sounds like an excellent idea." Wilhelmina folded her hands in her lap. "Would you mind if I went with you?"

"Of course not."

With her actions the last few weeks and her new desire to be a private detective, Wilhelmina seemed perfect for learning self-defense. It would help her in the future. And perhaps Thea could help her with her future cases.

A man passed by the cafe. There wasn't anything particularly special about him. He was an older man of average height, wearing a well-tailored suit. But she couldn't shake the feeling that she knew him from somewhere.

"Where are you going?" Wilhelmina asked, her hand suddenly on Thea's arm. Until that moment, she hadn't realized she had stood up, nor that she had begun to walk towards him. "Thea? What is it?"

Thea nodded towards the man. Wilhelmina and James followed her gaze. "Do you know him?"

Thea shook her head. "He seems so familiar though."

Out of the corner of her eye, she saw Wilhelmina and James glance at each other and frown.

"We should follow him," Wilhelmina said suddenly.

Thea nodded. She wanted to know who he was. Why did she feel like she had seen him before?

Wilhelmina slid her arm into Thea's, keeping her grip on Thea's wrist so that she couldn't wander off. She felt like they were treating her a bit like a child, but after what happened the other day, she supposed she couldn't blame them. She would be wary too if it was one of them who had gotten hurt.

Thea guided Wilhelmina after the older man. James stayed back, giving them some space. They were able to get closer to the counters and pretend to shop, which allowed them to get near enough to the man that she could smell his cologne, the same citrus smell she remembered the day in the storeroom.

She looked to Wilhelmina, heart racing. What if he saw

her? Would he recognize her? Would he know it wasn't Molly who he had pushed that day?

Her chest felt tighter than it had in ages. Every inch of clothing pressed against her skin. It didn't make sense. It fit this morning when she put it on. Why was it too tight now? Why was—

"Thea," Wilhelmina whispered, prying Thea's fingers loose from her arm. "Breathe."

What a strange thing to say. She was breathing. She was just breathing too fast. She knew it needed to slow down, but she couldn't figure out how.

She closed her eyes, trying to shut out everything. Wilhelmina put a hand on her shoulder, and Thea tried to focus on that. She took a breath and held it until her lungs hurt, then let it go. Another breath, then again. The knot seemed to loosen, so she opened her eyes.

Wilhelmina stared at her, face full of concern. "Is that him then?"

Thea nodded, thankful that Wilhelmina didn't ask her if she was all right. Instead, Wilhelmina handed her a handkerchief so that she could dab at the tears that had welled up in the corners of her eyes. She heard Wilhelmina say something to James, but she didn't pay much attention, trying to focus on breathing evenly and steadily. She knew from past experience if she didn't concentrate on this, she would spiral into another set, and it could go on for hours.

She closed her eyes once more, took another breath, then opened them.

"We need to let the police know," James was arguing, his hushed voice drawing attention from the girl behind the counter. When she saw Thea watching her, she looked away quickly.

Thea sighed and turned back to see if she could spot the man again. It took a few moments, seconds in which she could feel the panic start to bubble up again that they might have lost him, but she eventually found him talking to two of the employees. The body language between the two of them was familiar. He seemed to know who they were, and they both seemed comfortable with him. The man waved his hand, and another stopped by, answering his questions as well.

Thea turned back to the girl who was working behind the counter. "Excuse me?"

The girl paused, lifting her head. "Yes, ma'am?"

"Do you know who that man over there is?"

The girl's brow furrowed. "That man? That's Mr. Warwick."

"Who's Mr. Warwick?"

"He is part of the board that runs the store, ma'am. He was supposed to take over when Mr. Talbot died." She smiled. "He's in here all the time."

"I didn't see him come out of the board meeting earlier."

The girl frowned. The young woman from the other day, the one that found her in the storeroom, stepped over with a hat in her hands. "He's been down here for a little while. I overheard him say he left the meeting early."

James was right. The police should be called.

It was, of course, at that moment that the man, Mr. Warwick, seemed to feel her eyes upon him. He looked over to her, face tightening in recognition.

Thea swallowed hard as he started to come towards her. Thea turned, walking back towards Wilhelmina and James.

"He's behind me," she told them as she walked by. She didn't dare risk stopping. Not when he would likely catch her if she stopped. Who knew what he would do to her? She doubted he wanted anyone to know he had attacked her, so it was best if he didn't realize that James and Wilhelmina knew as well. She hoped they would call the police.

She didn't slow down, quickening her steps as she led him away from others and into the back.

"Come back here! I only want to talk."

She didn't like the sound of that.

Once through the downstairs doors, she broke into a run, pulling up her skirts so she could run unencumbered. His footsteps grew louder as he came closer. Thea raced through the storeroom, barely pausing to pull the door to the loading yard open.

Why hadn't Wilhelmina and James caught up to them yet?

Immediately, she spotted Mr. Turner in his laborer's clothes. A crowbar was in his hands as he worked on opening the crates that sat stacked there.

"Please! There's a man right behind me. He's chasing me! He's going to hurt me," she begged Mr. Turner.

It was at that moment that Mr. Warwick came through the door. Mr. Turner didn't even hesitate, swinging the crowbar into the man's stomach.

It took a few minutes before James and Wilhelmina found them standing over the unconscious man. James reached for a piece of rope, tying Mr. Warwick's hands only seconds before Leslie reappeared with a couple of uniformed police officers.

"I had a bad feeling," he told her sheepishly. "I suppose it wasn't unjustified, but you do seem to have a handle on it."

"I appreciate your concern." She smiled at him, her cheeks feeling a bit warm as he studied her face.

"He didn't harm you, did he?"

She shook her head. "He might have, if Mr. Turner hadn't been here."

Leslie offered his hand to Mr. Turner, who shook it. "Thank you for keeping her safe."

"You're welcome, Inspector."

The two uniformed officers lifted Mr. Warwick from the ground. He seemed awake, but groggy and Thea could only feel thankful that he hadn't been alert when she was alone with Mr. Turner. A crowbar might not have stopped him a second time.

"I need to go, take him into custody. You're sure you are all right?"

Thea nodded. "I am."

"Can I call on you later?"

She blushed, ducking her head even as she nodded. "Of course."

He gave her hand a squeeze and walked away.

"Well!" Wilhelmina exclaimed. "That was quite a bit of excitement for one day. Wouldn't you agree?"

"I would."

She was glad he had been captured, but it would be a while before she felt safe again.

CHAPTER TWENTY

It was a dinner party consisting of the six of them that night. She wanted to invite Mr. Turner, but he had turned her down, not feeling like it was appropriate. Her mother was out for the evening at another dinner party, so tonight was the perfect time for it.

"Inspector Haddington and I have been interviewing Mr. Selkirk and Mr. Warwick," Leslie said. "Warwick confessed to the attacks on Mrs. Talbot. That day in the storeroom, he mistook Thea for Mrs. Talbot. He was sure that he was going to get Daniel's position heading the store until Molly came along. He thought if he could scare her, she would step down and he would get the position."

Lionel's hand tightened on his glass. "And Selkirk?"

"Confessed to killing Mr. Turner. Turner had been black-mailing him about—" Leslie hesitated and Lionel nodded.

"He's been the one stealing the money from the store then?"

Leslie nodded. "He had been slowly poisoning Mr. Bexley for months when they would take tea. He wanted to make it look like Bexley had just gotten sick. And it might have worked if his"—he glanced at Lionel—"co-conspirator hadn't…"

"Killed Daniel and framed Lionel?" Molly finished. Leslie nodded again.

Lionel and Molly didn't stay long after dinner finished, but Thea, James, Wilhelmina, and Leslie adjourned to the drawing-room for drinks. Thea had never been very social, preferring to avoid situations when she had to be too social. As a result, her circle of friends had always been quite small and she never really had nights like this. It was nice to be with an intimate group of friends who knew her so well.

Going to the side table where she had placed them earlier, Thea offered James the stack of notebooks. "This is everything I have. From the last few months." His brow furrowed. "I changed details. It's not exactly the same. But I was wondering if you thought anyone might enjoy reading them."

James smiled. "I'll read them."

"Writing runs in the family, then?" Wilhelmina teased. Thea flushed, even as she laughed along with the others. It felt good to be so carefree for a change, free of worrying what others might think if they got too close and didn't like what they saw.

They spent hours talking and playing cards. Wilhelmina put a record on the gramophone and pulled Thea into a dance. The two of them spun around the room, neither of them really leading until Wilhelmina pulled Leslie to his feet and dragged James out to dance with her.

Leslie's hand was firm around hers. His other rested gently on her waist. She could feel it through her dress, pressing her closer as they swayed to the music. Her eyes started to drift shut, and she wondered what it might be like to lay her head on his shoulder and let him lead her around the room.

"You look like you might fall asleep on your feet," Leslie whispered, his eyes bright.

"I might. It's been a long day."

The room seemed quieter and it took her a moment to realize that James and Wilhelmina had both disappeared. When had they left?

"It is getting late. I should probably go."

He began to withdraw but she held his hands tightly between hers. "I don't want you to leave yet."

He watched her and her breath caught in her throat. For a moment, she thought he might go. But then he stepped closer. His head dipped as her face lifted and he pressed his lips to her cheek ever so gently. If she were to turn her head, he might be kissing her properly. But she stayed still and let him pull away. He hesitated, eyes watching her intently, and she wondered if he was waiting for a sign.

"Good night, Thea. I'll see you soon."

His hands left hers, and he walked out the door.

CHARACTERS
THEA'S FAMILY

Lady Theodora Prescott-Pryce – Thea lives with her widowed mother in London. Her younger brother, Cecil and his wife, Ilene, live at the Astermore Manor in Yorkshire.

Mercury - Thea's mischievous black kitten that she found at Ravenholm Castle.

Vivien Astermore - The Dowager Lady Astermore - mother of Thea and the current Earl of Astermore.

Apollo and **Artemis** - the Countess' Blenheim Spaniels.

James Poyntz – a journalist for the *West End Gazette* and Thea's half-brother.

———

Detective Inspector Leslie Thayne a.k.a. the Honorable Edward Leslie Thayne – the younger son of a Scottish Baron and works in the Criminal Investigation Department of Scotland Yard.

Mrs. Wilhelmina Livingston – Thea's friend and an American heiress.

Detective Inspector Thomas Haddington - a police inspector who works with Leslie.

Detective Constable Patrick Cooke - met Molly while he was working undercover.

Fletcher's Department Store

Mrs. Margaret Talbot - formerly Lady Thea's maid, widow of the late Daniel Talbot, and co-owner of Fletcher's Department Store.

Mr. Lionel Fletcher - Board member and co-owner of Fletcher's Department Store.

Richard and Victoria Talbot - Daniel's parents, members of the board.

Mr. Richard Selkirk - one of the board members.

Mr. Hervey - one of the board members, insistent that Molly retire. Mr. Turner works for him.

Mr. Charles Turner - secretary for Mr. Hervey. His twin brother John works in the loading docks.

Mr. Warwick - one of the board members, was supposed to take over the store when Daniel died.

Mr. Peter Bexley - the late head accountant for Fletcher's, was married to Thea's former finishing school friend Louise Radcliff.

Staff at Prescott House

Bridget Semple - Thea's new lady's maid who traveled with her from Scotland.

Mr. Albert Morgan - butler.

Nellie Davis - parlor maid.

Ezra Jones - chauffeur and footman.

ALSO SET IN THEA'S WORLD:

An Invitation to Tea: A Historical Romance Novella

<u>**A Lady Thea Mystery**</u>

Book 1: Murder on the Flying Scotsman

Book 1.5: The Unread Letter

Book 2: The Corpse at Ravenholm Castle

Book 3: A Most Fashionable Murder

Book 3.5: A Christmas Puzzle

A Prescott House Mystery

Book 1: Murder at the Midnight Ball

When a bright young man teams up with a glamorous courtesan, the identity of a murderer won't be the only secret they'll unmask.

London, 1922. Between gallivanting in his Rolls-Royce and darkening the doorways of London's hotspots, Lord Reginald "Rex" Bankes-Fernsby has almost succeeded in banishing the battlefield nightmares that plague his sleep. Pity he can't say the same about that nagging lack of direction in his life.

If only he were like his best friend Freddie - self-assured, suave, and up to his ears in secrets. But when Freddie is murdered, Rex doubts the verdict. Was Freddie really cut down while up to no good or was he killed in the line of duty?

Rex turns to the only person in London capable of helping him find out - Theodora Laurent, London's famous courtesan and Freddie's last known lover.

Theodora has a hundred reasons to let sleeping cats lie, but those disappear into the aether when Rex shows up on her doorstep and someone takes a shot at her head. Together, they're catapulted into a race for their lives, where identifying the murderer is their only hope for survival.

There's just one problem. Freddie wasn't the only one keeping secrets. If Theodora isn't careful, Rex's search for the truth could send her cunningly constructed empire falling like dominos.

———

Check out Lynn's other books by visiting:
https://lynnmorrisonwriter.com/

ABOUT THE AUTHOR

Named for the famous fictional mystery writer Jessica Fletcher, Jessica Baker picked up a pen when she was in elementary school and never set it down.

Jessica lives in sunny Central Florida and is a member of the National Sisters in Crime. When she's not writing, she works at a university and freelances as a camera assistant in film which provides plenty of inspiration for her stories.

To learn more about Jessica and her books, visit her at www.jessicabakerauthor.com and for the latest information, subscribe to her newsletters.